THE BIG BOOK OF ADULTING LIFE SKILLS FOR TEENS

A Complete Guide to All the Crucial Life Skills They Don't Teach You in School for Teenagers

EMILY CARTER

TABLE OF CONTENTS

Your Free Gift. . . . .*v*

Introduction *1*

Part 1: Living Away From Home   4

Chapter 1: Renting and Moving. 5

Chapter 2: Cooking and Meal Planning. 15

Chapter 3: Cleaning and Organization 23

Chapter 4: Home Maintenance and Repairs 27

Part 2: Financial Literacy   38

Chapter 5: Healthy Finances Are the Foundation of a Happy Life. 39

Chapter 6: Credit Scores, Credit Cards, and Debt. 49

Chapter 7: Investing and Planning for the Future 57

Part 3: Relationships and Communication   66

Chapter 8: Different Relationships, Same Foundations . . 67

Chapter 9: Developing Healthy Communication Skills. . . 77

Part 4: Health and Wellness 88

Chapter 10: Physical and Mental Health Go Hand-in-Hand 89

Chapter 11: Self-Care and Healthy Habits. 97

Chapter 12: Medical Matters. 109

Part 5: Personal Development 116

Chapter 13: Time Management and Goal Setting 117

Chapter 14: Growth Mindset, Self-Confidence, and Resilience 131

Conclusion *139*

About The Author. *143*

References *145*

YOUR FREE GIFT

Having the right mindset is the key when it comes to achieving success in any area of your life. As a way of saying thank you for your purchase, I want to offer you my book *Unleashing Your Potential: A Teenager's Guide to Developing a Growth Mindset and Opening Your Path to Success* for completely FREE of charge.

To get instant access, just scan the QR-code below or go to: https://lifeskillbooks.com/life-skills-free-bonus

Inside the book, you will discover...

✧ The difference between a fixed and growth mindset, how your mindset impacts your personal growth and success, and why a growth mindset is the one you should adopt.

✧ Practical strategies to cultivate a growth mindset, from daily habits to overcoming obstacles.

✧ How to utilize a growth mindset to supercharge your academic and career success.

✧ And much more!

But wait, there's more to come...

In addition to the *Unleashing Your Potential* eBook, I want to give you two additional special bonuses:

BONUS 1

The Essential Summer Job Handbook: The Teen's Guide to a Fun and Profitable Summer

Inside this exciting guide, you will discover...

✧ The many benefits of having a summertime job, from earning extra cash to gaining valuable experience and skills that will set you up for success in the future.

✧ The different types of jobs available for teens at different ages, and how to market yourself effectively to potential employers.

✧ Practical tips for avoiding being taken advantage of, and advice on tax considerations that every working teen needs to know.

BONUS 2

Raising Teens With Confidence: 10 Exclusive Blog Posts on Parenting Teens

I know this sounds boring if you're a teen, and that's completely fine. But for you parents out there, these unreleased blog posts offer a great opportunity to learn some new effective ways of parenting your teen.

Inside this compilation, you will discover...

✧ Invaluable insights and practical tips on how to navigate the challenges of parenting teenagers, from setting boundaries and dealing with mood swings to managing serious issues like drink and drug use.

✧ How to pick your battles wisely and let go of the small stuff, while still maintaining a strong connection with your teen and encouraging them to open up to you.

✧ Effective strategies for getting your teen to help out more at home, and how to strike the right balance between being a supportive parent and allowing your teen to develop their independence.

If you want to really make a change in your life for the better and get ahead of 95% of other teens, make sure to scan the QR-code below or head to the web address below to gain instant access to your bonuses.

https://lifeskillbooks.com/life-skills-free-bonus

INTRODUCTION

For in every adult there dwells the child that was, and in every child there lies the adult that will be.

–John Connolly

The moment my parents drove away after dropping me off at my college dorm was a shock to my system. It was at that moment that I realized I was alone. I was responsible for myself, from what and when I'd eat to what time I'd go to bed at night. It was at that moment that I realized I'd made it. I was an adult with adult responsibilities.

In my sophomore year, when I opted to rent an apartment with a friend near campus, I realized that I'd been wrong. Living in a dorm is like adulthood on training wheels. You have a meal plan and dining halls. There are Resident Assistants (RAs) there to help with conflicts with roommates or other problems. In your own apartment or house? You're responsible for it all, from cleaning and cooking to making sure all the bills you've never had to think about before are paid.

Moving away from home for the first time is a big deal. Whether you're leaving the nest for a dorm for the school year or choosing an apartment, it's a big responsibility. From renting and moving to keeping yourself fed and your home organized, there's enough to consider to make your head spin, and don't worry—that's normal. This is your first major step into independence and adulthood. Once you move, you'll be responsible for feeding yourself, keeping your home clean, and doing maintenance on your home and car. You won't have your parents to fall back on the second something goes wrong, and while you may be able to call them to ask for help, they probably won't be cooking and cleaning or doing your laundry for you.

The first time my apartment sink backed up, I had no clue what to do. It wouldn't drain, no matter how much I ran the garbage disposal. It wouldn't budge. I was equally clueless the time my car's tire blew out mid-winter one year until I was informed that the tire pressure was well under what it should have been.

There were so many things I didn't know about adulthood that, looking back, should have been taught in school. After all, if school is meant to prepare us for the world, why are we spending time memorizing the Pythagorean theorem instead of how to handle debt? Why aren't we taught how to take care of ourselves and our homes?

Ultimately, now as an adult, I understand the importance of teaching children how to *be* adults. That begins with an understanding of all the things you'll need to do living away from home.

That's why I put together this book. It's all about the skills I wish I'd learned sooner. I'm sure they would have saved me a lot of time learning via trial by fire. I don't regret the past or the struggles I faced growing up—they certainly taught me valuable life lessons that I've used to thrive later on. However, if I can save even one teen from making all those same mistakes or going into adulthood blindly, I've done my job.

As you read this book, you'll get a preview of what it takes to be an adult. This means being able to manage your own household and finances to managing your relationships and conflicts. You'll learn about keeping yourself healthy and also what it takes to have a mindset that will set you up for success.

Before you dive in, there's one thing I want to emphasize. You never stop learning, growing, or changing. Even if these things seem tough to remember or do at first, that doesn't mean you won't be able to do them later. You may be an adult or approaching adulthood, but that doesn't mean that you'll suddenly have all the right answers. You don't magically get any brand new insight the moment you hit adulthood. But, you do get handed a whole lot of new responsibilities as you prepare to set off on your own.

Approach these skills with an open mind and a willingness to learn, even if it takes you several tries to get something done. As long as you keep on trying, you'll get to where you want to go. After all, you haven't failed unless you've decided to give up or not participate at all!

PART 1

LIVING AWAY FROM HOME

Never underestimate the power you have to take your life in a new direction.

–Germany Kent

CHAPTER 1

RENTING AND MOVING

When it's time to move on to your own place, it's normal to feel nervous, excited, and maybe even a little bit scared. As you say goodbye to your parents and shut your door on them for the first time, it's strange. It's like shutting that door breaks a tether that's held you to them for your entire life. You entered this world knowing only them. You held their hand as you grew, watched them as they taught you, and lived with them your whole life, and now? You've left the nest.

It's a bittersweet moment for you and probably your parents too. They're probably brimming with pride as they drop their precious baby off for the last time, but they're probably also a little bit afraid, sad, and not quite ready to let go.

Whether you're moving into a dorm, a rental, or buying a house, there's always a huge transition shift when you finally walk out the door of your parents' home for the last time. There's a finality to it, but that doesn't have to be a bad thing. It just means you've grown up, and you're ready to start your own life. That's normal. It's only natural.

Of course, this comes with a little caveat—you suddenly find yourself responsible for all the things you probably took for granted growing up. Bills being paid, chores getting done, milk magically appearing in the fridge... These things take time and mental labor. And now? That's all yours. Congratulations!

But, before it's time to say goodbye and start your new life, you have to get somewhere to live first. Moving into a dorm is relatively simple for most people. You put in the application, you get assigned a room on campus, and you pay for it for the year. However, moving into an apartment on your own requires a lot more thought. From knowing lease terms to how to avoid a scam, there are some things to keep in mind.

Don't forget that your parents or guardians can be a major support during this process. They might cry when you get your first set of keys, but they can be just the people to turn to if you have specific questions. After all, they want what's best for you and they've got the experience to boot.

Everything You Need to Know

Before renting and moving, you'll want to familiarize yourself with several steps in the process. What are the terms of your lease? What utilities does the rent cover, if any? What about furniture and appliances? Why do you have to pay two or three months' rent upfront? Does renter's insurance really matter? Why? What is it? For a brand-new apartment hunter, there's a lot that you need to know that you may never have considered before, and that's okay! We all start somewhere and this is the perfect starting point.

Lease Terms

Leases are the contracts you sign when renting an apartment that grants you exclusive use of an apartment, room, house, or any other rental unit in exchange for an agreed-upon price. They're more than just that, though. They also list out the rules and guidelines that you need to abide by while renting, and if you violate the terms of the lease, you may break the contract and lose your right to remain in the unit.

Each lease will be different, so you'll want to read it all prior to signing it and ask any questions about terms you're unsure about or don't understand. The leasing agent will be able to walk you through it all.

Keep in mind that leases will also vary around the world. While in the US, it's standard for leases to include appliances; other countries may give you an entirely empty unit without a fridge, cabinets, or counters. While in the US, you can expect to have a background check run, be required to verify your income, and provide valid identification; other countries may also have additional requirements. You may be required to provide structural repairs in other countries as well.

Another thing to remember is that your lease will likely dictate whether you're allowed to have long-term guests to prevent unintended residencies. In many places, someone residing in a unit for longer than a month is enough to establish tenancy, even if they're a guest, and that can create a lot of legal headaches for the landlord if they refuse to leave. Even without a valid lease for that long-term guest, they may be forced to legally evict them if they can prove they've been there long enough.

Are Utilities Included?

Sometimes, utilities are included in your rental costs. This is especially common if you rent a room in a house. However, most rentals in the US will require you to have utilities in your own name, including electricity, gas, water, sewer, and garbage. You'll also likely have to pay for your own internet costs. Verify what's included in your lease beforehand to avoid any surprises, such as having to have the utilities transferred prior to moving in.

Deposits and Move-In Costs

Before you move in, you'll usually be responsible for the first month of rent. This seems pretty straightforward, right? Well, there are other expenses that will likely come into play too. Most rentals will charge a security deposit for any damages beyond normal wear and tear, which is any expected damage accrued by regular use, such as a wobbly doorknob or scuffs and wear on flooring.

The exact amount of your deposit will depend on what the state or country allows. For example, in Seattle, where I live now, a landlord can't charge more than one month's rent for a security deposit or nonrefundable fees, and renters have up to six months to pay off the security deposit, nonrefundable fees, and the last month's rent in a payment plan. This is a city-specific regulation, while the state of Washington has no such cap. Colorado has no caps on security deposits. Connecticut allows two months' rent for most tenants, but for those 62 or older, that number is halved to the equivalent of one month.

Make sure you know what's considered a legal deposit in your location prior to signing a lease and remember, if the deposit doesn't seem to align with what the law allows, there's a chance you're walking into a scam.

Beyond the deposit and last month's rent, you may also be required to pay a pet deposit or pet rent, deposits to begin utility services in your name, or other fees that may be dictated in your lease. You may also have to pay for movers, rent a moving truck, or pay someone to help you to get your belongings where they need to go.

Renters Insurance

Your lease may or may not require that you keep a renters insurance policy, but even if it's not obligatory, it's still a good idea to have. Renters' insurance typically covers unexpected events, which in the insurance world are known as covered perils. Each policy will vary in both coverage and cost, so make sure you speak with an agent who can help you understand which plans will work best for you. It typically comes with three types of coverage:

✧ **Personal Property:** This covers the cost to replace or repair any of your belongings that have been damaged, including furniture, electronics, and other items, up to the limit of your policy.

✧ **Liability:** This covers the cost of repairs if you accidentally damage the property or the cost of medical bills for a guest if they are injured on the property and you're found responsible, up to the limit of your policy.

✧ **Additional Living Expenses:** This covers any costs you may incur if your rental is damaged and you have to stay in a hotel.

Of course, there will be additional terms that will vary from company to company and state to state, such as what your deductible (the amount you pay before insurance pays out) will be, your premiums (the amount you pay monthly), and any covered perils.

Pet Policies

Pet policies can vary wildly, from allowing any and all dogs or cats to restricting you to specific sizes or prohibiting certain breeds. If you have a pet, this is probably one of the first considerations to make. Be sure to check your lease for pet policies, including a pet deposit, monthly pet rent, and any restrictions the property may have.

If you think you can get around the pet fees by hiding your pet, think again. This is a violation of your lease and you can be evicted and charged fees for pet damage. Likewise, if you have an apartment that doesn't allow pets at all, don't try to hide them.

Do You Need a Cosigner?

As a young adult, you'll likely start out without much credit unless your parents have been actively building it for you (more on this later). This means that you won't always look like the most attractive prospective tenant to landlords and they may be hesitant to rent to you since you won't have any sort of rental history. That's where cosigners come into play.

A cosigner is someone who co-signs your lease and agrees to be responsible for any fees, unpaid rent, or damages if you don't pay them. Typically, your cosigner will be someone with a much more established credit history and financial position, like your parents. Just remember that the cosigner is also on the lease and will have the same access to the property as you will. An alternative to a cosigner is a guarantor, who promises to pay the rent if you don't but does not have access to the apartment.

Choosing a Rental

If it's time to begin your rental search, hold your horses. Before you get too excited and start circling all the chic rentals with a million amenities and upgraded features, you've got some planning to do. I know how tempting it is to scroll through available units and dream of your new life in the best of the best, but the reality is most of us start small and work our way up. Choosing a rental takes a whole lot of planning, research, and time, and even then, you may not get the first one you apply for.

What's Your Budget?

The biggest factor in the entire apartment search is your budget. After all, you have to be able to afford your new place. Getting in over your head, even if you may qualify for an apartment that is, on paper, unaffordable, is a good way to start on the wrong foot.

Generally speaking, your budget should be less than 30% of your monthly income. This is where things get tricky, especially with the housing and rental markets skyrocketing. If you're making the U.S. minimum wage of $7.25 per hour while working a full-time job, that puts your annual pay at

$15,080, or an average of about $1,257 per month. Using the 30% rule, you can only afford to pay about $377 per month in rent.

If that's looking bleak to you, you understand exactly what problem so many young adults of today face, and that's being unable to afford to live alone. If your pay alone is not enough to cover the average cost of rent in your area, you have some options. The most popular one is to rent with friends or roommates and everyone contributes to the monthly cost. This can make rent more affordable. Alternatively, you may need to consider living with parents or family members while gaining work experience, going to college, or pursuing a trade to boost your earning power.

To calculate your budget, take your hourly pay and multiply it by the number of hours you work per week. Then, multiply that number by 52 (for 52 weeks in the year to get annual pay). Divide that number by 12 to get your monthly average income. Then, multiply your monthly average income by 0.3 to see what the most you should be paying for rent is.

What Do You Want or Need?

Once you know how much you can pay, you can start considering amenities that matter to you. Start with a list of all the things you need out of your home, such as the distance to where you work or go to school and non-negotiable amenities.

- ✧ **Parking:** If you drive, you probably want somewhere that has available parking. Some apartment complexes may have assigned parking spots.

Others may not offer any parking at all and require you to park on the streets.

✧ **Neighborhood:** Do you have a particular neighborhood you're partial to or neighborhoods you'd like to avoid? Check out crime statistics in the area you're considering, and spend some time looking around the area in person if you can to get a good feel for it.

✧ **Amenities:** Are there any amenities that you absolutely must have? For many, appliances like dishwashers and washers and dryers are required. Others may consider having an on-site gym or pool essential.

✧ **Closeness to work or school:** What is the farthest you're willing to move from your work or school? Remember, even if prices are cheaper for you to live further away, you may be spending so much more on transportation that it's actually more expensive than living closer.

Make a Short List

With your list of wants and needs and with your budget, you can then go searching for vacancies. Make a list of three to five rentals that you'd like to check out, that you can afford, and that meet your list of needs. You can search for rentals through word of mouth, asking around if anyone knows of vacancies, or online. Check out local property management companies to see if they have anything that will work for you.

View Apartments

Contact the apartments on your shortlist and ask if you can schedule a tour. It's strongly recommended that you never rent a place sight unseen because there may be problems that aren't obvious in photographs online. Take the time to tour the units and neighborhoods, and if you can, bring a trusted, experienced adult to take a look at everything, too.

Apply

Once you've decided on an apartment in your budget that meets your needs, it's time to apply. Be aware that most places will have non refundable application fees to cover background checks, and applying isn't a guarantee you'll get the place, especially in areas with a lot of competition. If your application is accepted, make sure you review the lease carefully before signing it.

Chapter Summary

Getting your first place is probably going to feel a little overwhelming at first. After all, you have to figure out what you need and can afford and then find somewhere with the availability that works for you. It might be with roommates, or you may truly be on your own for the first time. Either way, these tips are meant to try to smooth out the process. Don't forget that you can always ask for help from people around you!

And, once you've got your very own place to call home, you get to experience something new—managing your diet. From cooking to meal prepping, the next chapter will dive into everything you need to know.

CHAPTER 2

COOKING AND MEAL PLANNING

W e all need to eat at some point. Once you've settled into your new place, that responsibility falls firmly on your plate. Or, you might have roommates and decide to split up the responsibilities. Either way, there's no more Mom or Dad taking care of this for you, so it's time to get comfortable in the kitchen if you're not already.

I had roommates at one point and we rotated between cooking and cleaning on various nights. I've also had roommate situations where we were each responsible for feeding ourselves and cleaning up our messes after using the kitchens. You'll want to hash out expectations with your roommates before moving in together so you're on the same page. Will some items be free for everyone to use? Will you have different shelves in the fridge and cabinets for your food? These are all considerations to make.

Then comes meal planning, shopping, and keeping yourself satisfied, hopefully with healthy foods.

Dive Into Meal Planning

Meal planning is one of those things that sounds intimidating but is far easier than most people think. It's all about setting up a calendar with what you'll eat and when and making sure you have all of the ingredients on hand. This can really help you if you're the kind of person who gets overwhelmed with choices and doesn't know what to make, so you end up choosing to order out or buy something easy, which can be a big drain on your budget.

Meal Planning Steps

Meal planning really is as easy as following four simple steps that will keep you on track and help you to stretch your budget while still eating healthy foods that will keep your body running. If you reach for empty carbs and snacks like potato chips when you're busy and hungry, you aren't doing yourself any favors. You'll be hungry again a short while later. With meal planning, especially if you prep your meals in advance, you'll always know what's available and have something easy to eat.

Step 1: Take the Time to Plan

Each week, dedicate an hour or two to planning your meals for the next week. Try to plan breakfasts, lunches, and dinners. If you know there are days in your schedule when you're busy, make sure you have quick meals for them. Write down the meals and ingredients you'll need to make them.

While you're at it, choose meals that use similar ingredients so you can buy in bulk and lower costs. For example, maybe you make a chicken stir fry one night and then chicken fajitas the next. This lets you use up everything without waste.

Step 2: Check What's Already in the Kitchen

Once you have a list of ingredients, check your kitchen to see what you already have. Make sure that you check the use-by dates to ensure everything is still good, and if you have any ingredients that are about to expire, consider altering your meal plan to include those foods to avoid waste.

Step 3: Make Sure You Like the Meals

The key to sticking to a meal plan is making sure you're excited to eat the food. If you decide on recipes to use up items that you don't really like much, you'll be more tempted to ignore them and order in.

Step 4: Cook in Bulk and Use Your Leftovers

Choosing meals that make multiple servings can help make your meal-planning process easier. Even better, you can use the leftovers for lunch the next day. Just make sure that any meals that you choose to cook in bulk will reheat easily.

If you like big casseroles or dishes that usually result in a lot of food, you may be able to freeze them too. Foods like pot pies, casseroles, lasagna, spaghetti sauce, and stews all tend to freeze well, and you'll be able to pull out servings for lunches or dinners on busy days.

A Well-Stocked Kitchen is Key

Part of meal planning successfully is relying on some essentials in the pantry and fridge. When you first move to your first place, there are some things you should just keep stocked if they're part of your usual rotation of foods. These include:

Pantry Goods	Refrigerator Goods	Freezer Goods
Rice and grains	Milk	Frozen meats
Pasta	Butter	Frozen vegetables
Canned meats	Cheese	Frozen potatoes
Potato flakes	Eggs	Frozen fruits
Snacks	Yogurt	
Veggie and chicken broth	Fresh fruits and veggies	
Jarred peppers and olives	Meats	
Cream soups	Condiments	
Oils		
Flour		
Sugar		
Salt		
Baking soda		
Baking powder		
Seasonings		
Dried herbs		

A good way to help build up this stockpile is to buy in bulk when there are good sales and put items in your freezer. For example, maybe there's a good sale on chicken, so you buy more than you'd normally need and vacuum seal the extras to put in your freezer. This is a great way to cut down your costs.

Sprucing Up Cheap Meals

While ramen is hardly a balanced meal on its own, it's also one of those go-to foods that young adults eat regularly. After all, it's cheap, filling, and can be pretty tasty, too. I get it! I've had more than my fair share of instant noodles over the years.

When you go for cheap meals, there's no reason you can't spruce them up a bit. Toss in some frozen mixed veggies, a hard-boiled egg, and some chicken, and you've got a full meal. You can do this with other meals, too, like tossing vegetables into pasta or making fried rice with leftovers.

Meal Planning Tips for Young Adults

If you're planning out your weekly meals and trying to keep to a strict budget, you've got some options. These are some of my tried-and-true tips that I use to keep my food costs down without sacrificing much in the quality department.

Shop With Weekly Ads and Coupons in Mind

When you sit down to meal plan, review all the weekly ads and coupons at the store or stores you plan to shop at. You might notice that certain meats go on sale at certain points in the month or catch some killer deals on produce that you can use to implement into your meal plan. You might even be able to add some meat to your stockpile if you plan accordingly.

Stretch the Proteins

Especially in the US, there's this idea that protein has to be the main part of a meal. While planning around a protein can be helpful, it doesn't have to be the main dish. For example, instead of making burritos with lots of ground beef, you can cut the beef with a can of whole black beans to make it go further.

Throwing proteins into casseroles or pasta dishes can also help them feel like they go farther. Meat, in particular, is expensive, but by mixing it with other foods, you may be able to get more out of it.

Reach for Filling Foods

Foods that fill you up should be the bulk of your diet. When you shop, that means looking for whole foods that are on the perimeters of most grocery stores. The center aisles tend to be full of other foods that won't be as satisfying. Stick to the produce, meat, dairy, and whole grain areas as much as possible.

When you're hungry, grab satisfying foods like nuts, whole veggies, and fruits. Pair a carb with a healthy fat to boost feelings of fullness. After all, when you're satisfied with healthy foods, you're not going to be reaching for so many snacks, which can get expensive.

Cook at Home Whenever Possible

Just because you decide to meal plan doesn't mean that you can't eat out from time to time. But you'll want to focus on your meals at home, giving you healthy meals without breaking the bank.

Have Easy-to-Grab Foods Available for Those Busy Mornings

I get it—mornings are busy. I skipped my morning meals way too much when I was younger. Why bother eating if I need to rush out the door when having breakfast means waking up earlier? Why not just pick up a coffee and pastry at my favorite cafe on my way? Why not just pick up something from one of the dining halls? Well, the problem with this is that it gets expensive quickly.

Breakfast is the most important meal of your day. It stabilizes your blood sugar, which can help you feel more alert and energetic throughout the day, which also reduces the chances you'll be tempted by that afternoon's unhealthy snack.

I recommend keeping some easy grab-and-go foods on hand so you can have a complete breakfast any time you're in a rush. I love keeping DIY breakfast burritos and sandwiches in my freezer, so all I have to do is pop it onto a plate and warm it up for a minute while I get my coffee going. It saves my wallet and keeps me satisfied and full throughout my morning.

Chapter Summary

As one of the most basic needs that you require, food and thinking about food will probably be a pretty major part of your life for the foreseeable future. That's why implementing meal planning can be so useful—it takes thinking about food out of the equation. With minimal time spent handling and planning your food, you'll be able to free up time for other important things, like chores and staying organized.

CHAPTER 3

CLEANING AND ORGANIZATION

One of the biggest shocks to my system when I moved into my own place was just how much work goes into maintaining it. A good, solid cleaning schedule is key to keeping a clean environment, and that requires discipline. When I first got my own apartment, I realized that my parents did a lot more than I initially thought. They kept the floors vacuumed and mopped. They kept the bathrooms clean and the living room organized. While I had chores that I was responsible for, they paled in comparison to the regular upkeep of a home.

The best way for you to maintain your home is to have a schedule for daily, weekly, and monthly chores so you know what you're doing and when. This helps to keep you accountable and builds a routine where the cleanup is completed.

A Place for Everything

Any time you bring something home, it needs to have a dedicated place. This is one of the easiest ways to keep clutter down. If you don't have room for something, then it probably shouldn't be brought home. When you finish using something, return it back to its designated spot.

If it Takes Five Minutes, Do it Right Away

How often do you make a small mess and then tell yourself that you'll get to it later? This is an easy trap to fall into, but all those quick, little jobs can build up over time until what should have been easy tidying up becomes needing a deep clean or a more extensive scrub-down of an area. For example, if you spill something on the counter, you might tell yourself that you'll clean it when you do the dishes. Sure, it's not a big deal, but if you do that with all the little messes you make throughout the day, they all add up to a longer cleaning session.

The rule I use and that I teach my children is that if a cleanup task only takes five minutes or less to do after making a mess, then do it right away. If you spill your coffee, wipe it up right away. By doing the little tasks as soon as they pop up, you help maintain the cleanliness of your home so your cleanup routine stays consistent.

Develop a Regular Cleaning Schedule

Setting up a regular cleaning schedule can feel a little too reminiscent of chore charts for some new adults, but that's kind of the point. The chore chart helps keep everything done on time and makes sure nothing slips through the cracks. In my home, we divide chores into three categories.

Daily	Weekly	Monthly
Make your bed	Scrub bathrooms	Wipe baseboards
Do the dishes	Mop	Wipe light switches
Wipe counters	Vacuum	Deep clean appliances
Tidy up clutter	Wash bedding	Replace filters
Take out trash/ recycling	Clean out fridge	Vacuum underneath furniture
	Dust surfaces	Clean windows and tracks
		Scrub out trash cans

Of course, you might have other chores that you need to take care of, too, like cleaning out cat boxes, water changes for aquariums, watering plants, or yard work. Fit those in as needed as well.

From there, you have a few options. You can designate one day per week as your deep cleaning day or you can choose to do one or two weekly chores each day. For example:

✧ Sunday: Clean bedding and empty fridge

✧ Monday: Monthly chore

✧ Tuesday: Monthly chore

✧ Wednesday: Monthly chore

✧ Thursday: Dust surfaces

✧ Friday: Mop and vacuum

✧ Saturday: Scrub bathrooms

By adding in a few monthly chores on days you don't have weekly chores to complete, you can spread them out throughout the month so you don't find yourself overwhelmed on one or two days trying to get to everything on the list.

Chapter Summary

Keeping a tidy home can do wonders for your mental health, and it doesn't take much. Following these tips and setting a schedule can help you keep your home in tip-top shape—until something goes wrong and you have to fix it, that is. That's why the next chapter's here to prepare you with everything you need to know about maintaining your home—and which repairs to leave to the pros.

CHAPTER 4

HOME MAINTENANCE AND REPAIRS

The first time I had an apartment, I thought everything would be taken care of. After all, that's what maintenance is for, right? Well, there are a lot of maintenance things that the apartment isn't responsible for. Yes, they'll repair major issues with plumbing, dead appliances, and make sure that the environment is livable. You'll need to know what your responsibilities are and what your landlord is responsible for. Most of this is going to be dictated in your lease, outlining what you need to do.

Beyond when not to do your repairs, there are several common issues that you'll likely run into at one point or another that you'll need to be able to repair on your own.

When Not to Do Your Own Repairs

Some repairs are major and aren't your responsibility. In particular, these are habitable issues, problems with safety, or emergency requests.

✧ **Habitable issues:** If you have an issue that makes the environment uninhabitable, like issues with the electrical system, heating, air conditioning, or plumbing, these are usually concerns that maintenance will handle. Other issues include faulty appliances and pest infestations.

✧ **Safety problems:** Safety problems may include issues with smoke alarms, locks, or carbon monoxide detectors. While you may need to do battery replacements in alarms, your landlord has to make sure these devices function properly. Likewise, the entire property needs to be maintained. If there are trees outside that appear unstable, for example, the property owner has a duty to keep them safe.

✧ **Emergency requests:** Some emergency issues also warrant a call to maintenance for help. These include gas leaks, flooding, water leaks, or mold. If you notice these issues, you should contact maintenance and have them handle the situation.

How to Unclog a Drain

A clogged drain can really bring your daily routine grinding to a halt, especially if it's in your kitchen. However, other clogs can also occur, like in your toilet or bathtub. Thankfully, there are a lot of easy ways you can fix a clog without having to wait for maintenance.

Use a Plunger

A plunger is most commonly used for a toilet but can also be useful in other drains as well. Just be sure that any plunger used in your kitchen isn't shared with the toilet or make sure that it's thoroughly sanitized before using it. These work by forcing water down into the drain pipe to push the clog through and work well in many cases.

Use a Drain Snake

A drain snake or an auger is a long, flexible cable that you can use to push down a drain to pull out major clogs that you can't force through the plumbing with a plunger. With most of these, you simply put the coiled end into the drain and then turn the handle until it catches on something. Then, rotate it around to either catch the clog or break it apart. Recoil the snake and see if you pulled anything out, then flush the drain with hot water. If it's still draining slowly, you can repeat the process with the snake or move on to a liquid drain cleaner to chemically break down the clog.

Use a Liquid Drain Cleaner

Liquid drain cleaners are products you buy from the store that are poured down the drain to chemically break it down. They're great for breaking down clogs in drain systems, like hair or grease, especially in areas you can't easily reach the plumbing, like in a bathtub, but that also means that they can be dangerous if they get on your skin too. Make sure you follow the directions on the product's packaging to remove the drain and take care to avoid getting it on you.

Cleaning a Sink Trap

You may also be able to remove a clog by removing a sink's p-trap and then manually removing whatever is blocking it up. However, this can be messy, too, and you'll need to be careful to have a bucket or some other large container ready to catch any water stuck inside.

The p-trap is the u-shaped pipe underneath a sink and is designed to keep smelly sewer smells from coming through the pipes. This is usually done with a water seal, which means as soon as you remove it, water will spill.

To clean your p-trap, you'll need a flexible wire brush as well as pliers or an adjustable wrench, depending on the setup of your pipe. If you have a hard time visualizing the steps listed below, there are dozens of videos online that can also walk you through the repair step by step.

1. Turn off the water faucet and remember, even if the faucet is off, water will still leak once you remove the trap.

2. Many p-traps can be removed by hand. Twist the big nuts holding the p-trap onto the rest of the plumbing until it loosens. If it's tight, use a wrench or pliers. Be ready to catch the water because it'll start spilling as soon as the nut is loosened.

3. Once you've removed the p-trap, you can clean it out by pulling out any clogs. If needed, use a wire brush to force any clogs through the other end.

4. Put the pipe back into place and tighten the nuts again. Use the wrench or pliers if necessary to get a solid seal. Then run the water for 15–20 seconds to make sure there's no leakage from the nuts. If water

leaks, turn off the faucet and tighten the nuts before testing it again.

Cleaning the Garbage Disposal

Is your garbage disposal getting smelly? This is one of those appliances that you'll want to clean out at least monthly, but every week or every other week is often preferred. While garbage disposals see a lot of water pumping through them, there are areas that aren't easily rinsed clean when used, and that's what you'll need to clean.

It might seem daunting to stick your hand inside an appliance that exists just to break down foods, but you can remove the risk simply by turning off the power to the device at the breaker box. Before you begin, make sure you flip the switch to see if the disposal has been disabled. If it doesn't turn on, flip it off again, and then you can begin the cleaning process.

You'll need:

- ✧ a kitchen sponge
- ✧ a sink stopper
- ✧ dish soap
- ✧ ½ cup baking soda
- ✧ 1 cup vinegar
- ✧ ice cubes
- ✧ 1 cup rock salt
- ✧ water

✧ rubber gloves (if you want them)

Once you've got your tools handy and the power is off (this is important enough to repeat!), it's time to scrub.

1. Put on the gloves if you want to keep your hands clean, and then take the sponge and add dish soap to it. First, you'll want to scrub the baffle, which is the rubber part that leads down into the drain and keeps food from flying back up and out of the drain when using the disposal. Scrub it thoroughly, rinsing the sponge regularly to get rid of all the built-up gunk.

2. Use the sponge to clean out the grinding chamber, scrubbing the walls around the top and sides, and once again rinsing frequently until you stop seeing gunk come up on your sponge. This is enough for a weekly scrub of your disposal, but if it's extra stinky or it's been a while since you cleaned it thoroughly, you'll want to keep cleaning.

3. Dump the baking soda down the drain, then slowly follow up with the vinegar. Place the drain stopper over the drain to keep all the foam inside the garbage disposal, where it'll do its work. Leave it for at least 10 minutes. While waiting, go switch the power back on to the garbage disposal, and after the time is up, rinse the drain with hot water while running the disposal.

4. Turn off the disposal and fill up the drain with ice cubes. Dump in the cup of rock salt, then run the disposal to grind up the ice and salt. This will get any last bits of gunk left behind. Once the ice is ground

up, run some hot water to wash everything through, and your garbage disposal should smell fresh.

How to Clean Washers and Dryers

Washers, in particular, can start smelling dank if you don't take good care of them. The care for these will change based on whether you have a top-loading or front-loading washer. Front-loading washers tend to build up mold inside the door. The easiest way to prevent them from stinking is to remove wet clothes from them promptly and make sure you leave the door open when not in use to dry them out.

If your front-loading washer is starting to stink, you can wipe it down with a mix of 1:9 bleach to water solution and a small scrubber like a toothbrush. From there, the process of cleaning out any residue buildup is the same in both top- and front-loading appliances.

To clean it, you'll want to run a hot cycle with a cup of bleach on the long cleaning cycle. Then, run a second cycle with hot water and two cups of vinegar. Let it sit, then run another long cleaning cycle. Finally, run a long cycle with just hot water.

To be safe, you'll want to make sure the first load of laundry you do after bleaching your washer is just whites. I've learned this the hard way after turning my favorite pink shirt into a shell of what it once was, covered in bleached spots.

Dryers don't need as thorough of a cleaning since there are only clean clothes going into them, but lint can build up. Make sure you remove the lint trap and clean it out before every load of laundry to make sure that lint doesn't build up in the duct. This can be a fire hazard!

Try fitting a vacuum hose into the lint trap to suck out the remaining lint, then wipe out the drum with a mild detergent. You'll also want to clean the exhaust on the back of the dryer if you can. Loosen up the clamp on the back and use your hands to take out as much lint as you can. You'll want to shove your vacuum hose into this as well to suck out any remaining lint.

How to Clean Dishwashers

You might not know this but your dishwasher *also* needs to be cleaned frequently. Yes, the device that sanitizes your dishes can get dirty! If you've noticed that your machine isn't washing as well as it used to or you're getting funky smells coming from it, there's a good chance that the filter needs to be cleaned out. The good news is this is usually an easy cleaning process and with maybe ten minutes of active work, you can have it working as good as new.

You'll either want to have dishwasher cleaning products or baking soda and vinegar so you can break down any grease or soap scum stuck in the appliance.

1. Remove the racks, utensil holders, and the filter from the dishwasher. If you're unsure how, look up the model online or consult the instruction manual. The filter, in particular, will probably look pretty gross if you haven't cleaned it in a while. Scrub out the filter to remove any food, scum, or mold that

may have built up, then soak it in vinegar and warm water while you finish the rest of the scrubbing.

2. Wipe down everything you can see, including spray arms, side walls, and corners where gunk may have gotten stuck. Use a toothbrush or toothpick to get stubborn bits out.

3. Place the filter, racks, and utensil holders back into the machine and either use a dishwasher cleaning product on its own according to the instructions or set a bowl with a cup of vinegar into the bottom of the dishwasher. Run the cycle (sanitation cycle if you have it!).

4. After the vinegar cycle, remove the bowl and toss in a cup of baking soda across the bottom. This will deodorize the dishwasher and also remove any stains that may have gotten stuck. Run an express cycle with the baking soda and you're done!

How to Replace an Air Filter

Air filter replacements should happen frequently, every other month or so, or more often if you have pets or live somewhere that's dry and dusty. This is often a part of maintenance that you're expected to do on your own. You may have a reusable filter that needs to be vacuumed out from time to time, or you may need to replace it on your own. To change it, follow these steps:

1. Find the location(s) of your air filter. There may be more than one that needs to be changed.

2. Make sure you know the right size and get a new one. You'll need the right length, width, and thickness.

3. When you have the new filter, open up the housing and remove the old one. Wipe out any dust or grime from the housing and then place the new filter into the duct, paying attention to the arrows. Then, close the grille and secure it in place.

How to Replace Lightbulbs

If you have a lightbulb that doesn't turn on or is flickering a lot, it's probably time to replace it. Before you crack a joke about how many young adults it takes to change a bulb, know it's really simple. All you have to do is make sure you have the right light bulbs on hand, make sure the light is switched off and that the lightbulb is cooled off, then unscrew the old one and place the new one in.

If you have light fixtures, you may have to remove those first by unscrewing them to gain access to the bulbs. That's okay too! While you're changing your bulbs, consider picking up LED bulbs, which last much longer and are also energy-efficient and can lower your overall energy bill.

Chapter Summary

Doing basic maintenance on your home can be really intimidating if you were never taught to do it before, but it's not so bad after practicing it. Even better, knowing how to maintain appliances can actually help you to keep some money in your pocket instead of rushing out to replace them at the first sign of a problem or if you get a clog somewhere in your drain. Practice, check out tutorial videos online, and trust that you can learn and do these things just like other adults. After all, the handiest person around the house that you know once knew nothing about maintenance too.

With that money you save on repairs, you can throw it toward your savings. The next section of the book talks all about how to manage your finances and keep your spending under control while saving for the future.

PART 2

FINANCIAL LITERACY

Financial literacy makes it okay for you to make small or big mistakes. On the other hand, being financially illiterate only makes those mistakes dire and regrettable

–Anas Hamshari

CHAPTER 5

HEALTHY FINANCES ARE THE FOUNDATION OF A HAPPY LIFE

One thing I regret never being taught as a child and a teen is the value of saving money. It's easy to spend when it's sitting in your pocket or bank account, which makes saving all the more difficult when you know you have enough money to buy that new video game, phone, dress, or whatever else has caught your eye. As we'll talk about a few chapters from now, though, saving money, especially when you're able to grow it with interest, is one of the best things you can do for yourself, even if you have to give up a little bit for now to have it later.

While money can't buy happiness in the truest sense, in my experience, it's incredibly difficult to be happy *without* it. That doesn't mean that you need to strive for lavish vacations, designer brands, and partying it up without a care in the world to be happy, but feeling secure is difficult if you're scraping every last cent together to pay your bills or buy that cheap pack of ramen to have something to eat for the day. Having your finances in order means that you can alleviate some of that stress, and it all begins with budgeting. Through budgeting, you can save money and manage it better. The result? Less stress and more time to enjoy yourself, even if you're skipping out on that fun event everyone else is doing or not eating out as often as before.

The Basics of Budgeting

Budgeting is as simple as meeting three simple steps: Tracking your income, your expenses, and managing what's left over. The hard part is finding the willpower to stick to your budget. I personally manage my budget weekly and monthly using a spreadsheet with all of my family's expenses against the income we receive. Once per week, I tally up all of my expenditures and check them against my budget to make sure I haven't gone over.

Sure, my family gets by well enough that I don't have to count every last dollar or worry about whether I can buy something, but I've found that the only way to grow and *maintain* any wealth is through avoiding lifestyle creep and living well within our means. That means that sometimes, I tell my children no, we won't be going out to a restaurant for dinner when they request it. Could we? Sure. Should we? Not if we've already used our fun money for the week. Staying accountable and true to the budget is the best way that I've found to really help my family financially, and it's a skill I learned a decade later than I should have.

Your budget will help you understand exactly how much money you have for different things. If you decide to spend less in some categories, you may be able to free up additional cash to use elsewhere. For example, if you budget $100 for clothing every month but only spend $50, you've got $50 free that you can use on something fun or to put into savings.

Track Your Income

Income is any money that you have coming in that you can spend from all sources. Whether we're talking about money from a job, royalties, money you get refunded from student loans for living expenses, cash from your parents, or any other source, it's important to count it here so you'll know how much usable money you have. Start writing down all the sources of money you have, the amount you get, and how frequently you get it.

Make sure that, when counting money from jobs, you rely on the after-tax (net) income amounts since the taxes will likely be deducted immediately if you work a traditional job, or if you freelance, you'll have to pay those taxes at some point.

Once you have that number, hold onto it. It might not be as much as it looks like at first when you realize how much money you're spending. That's why it's so important to track your income.

Track Your Expenses

Next, it's time to track your expenses. Either write them down or put them into a spreadsheet for easy access. This will include recurring expenses, like any streaming subscriptions, credit card bills, rent, utilities, and car costs. It should also include a set amount that you spend on living necessities like food, clothing, haircuts, and similar budget lines.

Part of your budget should also include savings for emergencies, car repairs, or other unforeseen expenses. It should also include a line for money that you can use for fun.

With your spreadsheet ready to go, you can now track your expenses. Every week or two, you should sit down and check out all of the expenses from your bank account to see where you're spending money and then deduct that from the monthly allotments for those categories.

Once your budget of expenses is done, you can also begin a plan to save cash.

Pay Yourself First and Build Savings

No matter who you are or what your life plans are, having savings helps bring those goals to life. If you want to buy a house, you'll need healthy savings to do so. If you want to travel the world? You'll need money for that. Starting a business, paying off student debt, and generally just living life require money. Getting into good saving habits now means that it'll be easier to get to a comfortable position later.

One way to see this play out is in a 1960s psychology study by Stanford professor Walter Mischel. He studied the reactions of hundreds of children to determine their ability to delay gratification. The test involved setting a child in a private room with a marshmallow. The child was then told that the adult would leave the room and if the child didn't eat the marshmallow, they'd get two marshmallows later, but if they decided to eat the marshmallow while the adult was out, they wouldn't get the second marshmallow.

Some children ate the marshmallow immediately in the 15 minutes they were alone. Many others tried to wait but gave in a few minutes after. A few children were able to delay their urge to eat the marshmallow and got the second one. This is called delayed gratification—these children wait to enjoy more later.

Even more interesting, the children who were able to delay gratification also tested to have higher SAT scores, lower levels of substance abuse and obesity, and scored better in several other categories than their peers who didn't, including better stress responses and social skills. You can do the same thing with money.

Saving Money Now to Have It Later

If you learn to delay gratification, you get a wealth of benefits, and one of those is in your financial life. If you can turn down the invitation to that concert or choose to eat at home instead of going out, you can quickly build up cash savings that other people squander away on instant gratification.

The sooner you start saving, the less of your income you'll have to save just because your money will have more time to grow and accumulate interest, especially if you choose to invest it. It's recommended that you save 10–15% of your income for retirement if you start in your late teens or early 20s.

Emergency Savings

An emergency fund should be considered fully funded when you have enough in it to cover six months of expenses. Yes, this is probably a lot more than you'd expect, but it's important to have on hand. You never know if you'll get sick or hurt and need to take time off work, or you could lose or leave a job and need time to get a new one. This can also cover major expenses, like buying a new car if you suddenly need to replace it or covering the cost of medical expenses. Try to place at least 10% of your income into emergency savings.

Money Management Tips for Young Adults

Looking for some ways to manage your money and stick more into savings? These are some of my tried and true tricks to free up extra cash.

Skip the Debt. Pay with Cash

You pay a lot in credit card interest, which we'll discuss in the next chapter. Even if you only pay a minimum payment on a credit card, the final price of your purchases are inflated by interest. Pay with cash. If you can't afford it with cash now and it's not a necessity, don't buy it.

Stick to Your Budget

Your budget helps allocate every dollar you have so you know what's available to spend and what's already earmarked for something else. By making sure you stick to your budget, you can make sure that you hit your savings goals each month.

Manage Your Grocery Budget

Groceries are one of the biggest expenses we have. According to the U.S. Department of Agriculture, the average cost for groceries for one person is between $300 and $540 per month, but this can vary widely based on where you live and what kind of diet you eat. Make sure that you keep a close eye on the budget line and plan your meals to help manage your costs.

Consider Generic

Generic brands can help cut out a lot of extra costs. Those few cents between items can add up quickly, and often, generic food is just as good as the name brands. Figure out which foods you're happy to have the generic versions of and buy them to save money.

Coupons and Grocery Store Memberships

Coupons and memberships can help cut the cost of food as well. Make sure you're checking weekly ads and digital coupons to see what you can save, as well as signing up for grocery store loyalty discount memberships where you shop the most.

Cut Out the Subscriptions and Memberships You Don't Need

Do you really need three video or music streaming subscriptions? Are you actually using your gym membership or online gaming? These little subscriptions can be easy to sign up for since they're pretty cheap on their own, but they can quickly add up if you're not careful. Double-check any subscriptions you currently have and see if any of them can be cut out.

Transfer Money to Savings Automatically

Did you know that a lot of banks will allow you to transfer money to your savings account automatically? This is an easy way to put money out of sight immediately before it ever hits your checking account. Consider setting this up with your direct deposit if that's how you get paid.

Be Wise With Unexpected Income

Any time you get a sudden windfall, whether it's some cash for a holiday or birthday or you managed to win a sum of money. You could also wind up inheriting money, depending on your family setup, or getting a bonus at work. Be wise when you get unexpected income. Instead of running out to spend it, consider putting it into savings or investing it instead.

Pay Attention to Taxes

Part of being an adult is paying taxes. If, when you file your taxes, you receive a large tax refund, there's a chance your taxes aren't set up properly.

Spending Freeze

Have you ever heard of a spending freeze? It's a sort of challenge where you don't spend any extra money at all. Don't buy anything nonessential for a month and see how much cash you save.

DIY

While there are some things best left to the professionals, a lot of things can be done yourself, from sewing up minor tears in clothing to refurbishing furniture to give it a nice facelift.

Choose Secondhand Items

Buying things you need secondhand is a great way to pocket the extra cash that would otherwise go toward buying a boxed or brand-new item. While some things should be bought new for sanitary reasons, most things can be bought on secondhand marketplaces like Facebook Marketplace or Craigslist.

Chapter Summary

Making the most of your money is all about stretching your dollar as far as you can and building up savings so you're ready to cover any expenses that may arise. By managing your money, you can better get a handle on any potential debt you may accrue. In the next chapter, we'll be discussing how to safely use credit cards in ways that are beneficial to your financial health.

CHAPTER 6

CREDIT SCORES, CREDIT CARDS, AND DEBT

C redit—it's one of those things that you can't live without but building it can be dangerous. Part of building it requires you to take out loans and credit cards, but if you're not smart about how you use them, you'll do more harm than good.

As a young adult, you most likely won't have any credit, or if you do, it'll probably be pretty bad unless your parents helped you build it by adding you to credit accounts while you were younger to help you piggyback off their scores. Unfortunately, that makes it difficult for you to get housing, rent an apartment, or buy a car if you plan on using a loan. It can be hard to get credit cards, too, unless you know where to look.

This can make a loop where you can't take out lines of credit that won't put you at risk of serious interest payments, which means you can't build your credit easily. If you're like me, you'll fall into the trap of using credit cards as a sort of bridge between what you want and what you can afford. Don't do this! One of the worst things you can do is put yourself in debt over wants.

Credit Scores

If you live in the US, you have a credit score that's tracked by Experian, Equifax, or TransUnion. Many other countries have similar programs used to track creditworthiness that use similar factors in calculating a score.

In the US, this credit score is determined by considering several factors, including:

- ✧ **Debt owed:** The amount you owe versus how much available credit you have is a major component of your credit score. If you use most or all of your available credit, the assumption is that you are making ends meet with your credit because you don't have enough money to cover your monthly expenses, making you a higher risk for defaulting on future credit accounts.

- ✧ **New credit:** This considers how many accounts have been opened recently. People who have recently opened several credit accounts are usually considered a higher risk, so multiple new accounts can lower your score.

- ✧ **Length of credit history:** This is a tough one for young adults, but it's going to be helpful later. Credit scores are calculated in part by how long you've had credit, the age of your oldest account and newest account, and how long it's been since you've used accounts. The length of your credit history plays a part in calculating your score.

✧ **Credit mix:** This refers to the types of credit and loans you have, such as credit cards, installment loans (like cars or student loans), mortgages, and finance company accounts.

✧ **Payment history:** This is one of the biggest factors considered. All payments you make to your credit lines and loans are reported, and if you make them 30 days late or longer, they will be negative marks on your credit.

How to Judge Your Credit Score

Most credit scores range from 300–850, and those scores are divided into several categories that can give you a good idea of how your credit looks. These are:

✧ **Excellent:** 720–850

✧ **Good:** 690–719

✧ **Fair:** 630–689

✧ **Bad:** 300–629

We don't start out with a credit score—the first one is calculated based on your credit usage once you open your first line of credit. For many young adults, this is a student loan, but it may also be a credit card. Your first credit score will be calculated after having at least one credit account open and reporting to one of the three major bureaus for six months. Once you get your first account set up, make it count! Don't run out to celebrate that shiny new Visa card if you can't afford to pay it off.

What if You Miss a Payment?

If you miss a payment, a few things happen. One, you'll probably have some late fees associated with missing it. Two, if it's not paid within 30 days of the due date, it may be marked on your credit report as a missed payment, which will negatively impact your score. Some lenders don't report late payments until after 60 days past due, but you should still always pay your bills on time. Your late payments will remain on your credit report for seven years, which is why it's so important to avoid them whenever possible.

Credit Cards and Debt

Credit cards work by loaning you money to make purchases. In exchange, you owe the lender a debt that has to be repaid with interest. The interest amount will vary based on the terms of the card that you select. The vast majority of credit cards have a pre authorized limit based on your credit score. Many new cards start out with just a few hundred dollars but can go up into the thousands as your credit improves.

Carrying a balance on your credit card means that you owe money even after making the assigned payment, and that balance will be charged interest based on the annual percentage rate (APR) that you agreed to when taking out the card. Many cards use a variable APR that changes over time, and being 60 days late on your card can trigger a penalty APR, which will dramatically increase what you owe.

Some credit cards also come with fees, such as monthly and annual membership fees. While these cards often are easier to get with little or no credit, they're also incredibly expensive and you're essentially paying for the privilege of having it.

Other potential fees you may accrue include balance transfer fees, where you move the balance of one card to another, over-limit fees when you go over the card's credit limit, or late fees for missing the payment.

Credit cards aren't all bad, though. Many of them have perks that can make them worth using—wisely, of course. Credit cards tend to be safer than cash, coming with liability guarantees. It's often easier to dispute a credit charge than it is to fight a debit. Other benefits include:

- ✧ They're easy to use.
- ✧ Some offer rewards and cash back.
- ✧ They boost credit scores when used correctly.

On the other hand, before taking out a credit card and using it, be aware of the cons:

Interest and fees add up when you carry a balance.

They can harm your credit score if you carry a high balance or miss payments.

They make it easy to spiral into debt.

When Should You Use a Credit Card?

As dangerous as credit card usage can be, that doesn't mean that you should never use yours. Learning to use credit cards responsibly is the best thing that you can do for your credit score.

To Access a One-Time Bonus

Some credit cards will offer incentives for you to use them, such as offering a one-time bonus if you spend a set amount of money in the first few months the account is open. If you have an offer like this, using a credit card for your monthly expenses, like food and bills, allows you to then pay it off in full with the cash you'd normally use, avoiding the interest and earning access to the reward.

For Cash Back

Some cards also offer cash back for your purchases. If you have one of those cards, like with the one-time bonuses, you can build up cashback points. Some cards may offer up to 5 or 6 percent cash back on certain purchases, though they often have spending caps.

For Rewards Points or Frequent Flyer Miles

Other cards opt for rewards points or frequent flier miles when you use them. The more you spend, the more points you rack up, which can be used up later.

To Prevent Fraud

As we already discussed, credit cards are much easier to work with to fight fraudulent charges than when you pay with a debit card or cash. Because of this, your credit card offers a safe option for paying for your purchases.

This can also be used for making large payments toward vendors or handymen. If someone does a shoddy job, if you've paid with a credit card, you can get the charge reversed and have access to the money sooner rather than later. If subpar work is done after you've paid for it and you paid in cash, you run the risk of having to spend months fighting to claw back your money through legal avenues.

For Hotels or Car Rentals

If you plan to rent a car or stay at a hotel, you'll be required to use a credit card. This is just in case you cause damages.

Debt and Interest

Loans and credit card balances are considered debts, and they typically accrue interest. Interest rates on credit cards can vary wildly, with the average somewhere around 24 percent. That might not sound that bad, but it can get scary quickly.

Let's say you buy a new gaming console and accessories for $500 on a credit card with an average 24 percent APR. If you make your minimum monthly payment of $35, do you know how long it'd take you to pay it off?

By the time you pay it off in full with minimum payments, it will take 17 months. By the end, you'll have paid $82 in interest, adding that to the cost of the purchase. Is it worth it?

Interest is the cost of debt. It can be simple or complex, and most credit cards use compound interest, allowing it to accrue daily.

Simple Interest

Simple interest assigns the interest at the beginning of a loan at a set percentage. For example, a $100,000 loan with a 3 percent interest rate would have $3,000 in interest charged to it if the whole loan is paid off in a year. This is calculated by multiplying the principal (the amount of the loan) by the interest rate and by the number of years you'll be paying it.

Compound Interest

More commonly, especially with credit cards, you'll pay compound interest. This means that you'll pay interest on accruing interest as well as the principal. When you have to pay compound interest, you pay more over the long run because your balance owed grows while you pay it off. Some of each payment you make goes toward the principal, but the rest goes to pay off interest, meaning you're not paying it off as quickly as you'd probably think.

Chapter Summary

Credit cards might seem like a sudden windfall of fun money, but racking up debt is never a good idea. Even if you really want something, if you can't pay it off in full, you should wait until you can. Save on interest and save your credit score by using your credit wisely. This will help you to invest and plan for your future, which we'll discuss in the next chapter.

CHAPTER 7

INVESTING AND PLANNING FOR THE FUTURE

When you're just getting started in adulthood, it's easy to think that you've got plenty of time before you need to start worrying about retirement. After all, you have a whole career to build up money for your future financial security, right?

Well, the years go by much faster than you'd expect, and the sooner you start investing in yourself and your future, the more money you'll have, thanks to the very same interest you learned about in the previous chapter. When you invest and save, you can gain interest, allowing your money to work for you and grow while it sits. Having a savings account isn't enough to keep your money growing quickly enough to outpace inflation, either. Each year, your money has less buying power just because each year inflation pushes costs up. On average, the U.S. inflation rate is around 3.8 percent, though the COVID-19 pandemic caused it to increase significantly.

What that means is that your $100 one year is worth $96.20 the next, on average. If you leave your money sitting in a savings account, it loses value year after year, and the average interest rate in a savings account is around 0.39 percent. That's only 1/10 the inflation rate, meaning the longer your money sits, even in a savings account, the less spending power you'll have.

There are ways to get around this, and while I'm not delving deeply into these subjects, this will give you an overview of the options that you have. These options can help you safely build up money over time, and the sooner you set them up, the longer that interest can build. Remember this—a dollar that you save early will generate you more than a dollar saved later in life, thanks to the power of compounding interest.

For example, let's say you invest $1,000 right now in an account that has a 5% growth rate. This is how it will compound over the next 60 years:

Year	Total value of investment
0	$1,000
1	$1,050
2	$1,102.50
3	$1,157.63
4	$1,215.51
5	$1,276.28
10	$1,628.89
15	$2,078.93
20	$2,653.30

30	$4,321.94
40	$7,039.99
50	$11,467.40
60	$18,679.19

Looking at these numbers, you can see that they start to jump quickly. Look at the growth in terms of decades:

Period (years)	Growth
0–10	$628.89
10–20	$1,024.41
20–30	$1,668.64
30–40	$2,718.05
40–50	$4,427.41
50–60	$7,191.76

If you were to retire 50 years from now and invest $1,000 today, you'd have $11,467.40 with an annual compounding interest rate of 5%. If you were to wait 30 years from now and then invest $1,000, you'd only have $2,653.30 50 years from today in comparison. The initial investment would be the same, but that extra 30 years of compounding growth makes a big difference. This is why investing early is so important. The longer your money grows, the larger the growth becomes. Three of the best ways to grow your money are through life insurance (but only the right kind), investments, and retirement accounts.

Life Insurance

While life insurance is commonly seen as a way to provide for families in the event that someone dies, it's also a great way to grow money that you can use during your lifetime as well. It's a slower form of investment, but it's also the safest way to grow your money if you set up a policy correctly with the help of a licensed insurance agent.

Life insurance comes in two forms: term and permanent. Term policies are good for a set period of time and are cheaper. You pay into them, but they usually don't build cash value and they only pay out a death benefit if you die during the term you have them. This is great for families worried about making ends meet if they die while a spouse raises children because it provides a safety net while minor children are in the home.

Permanent life insurance is often more expensive, but it can also work to grow cash value that you can then borrow or withdraw while you're still alive. Because the cash value doesn't usually get added to the death benefit that pays out, the money that you invest and grow can be pulled out and used as a way to pay for retirement, investments, or other expenses. Even better, you can take that money out as a loan to avoid paying taxes on this money.

One consideration to make, though, is that if you overfund these life insurance policies, they can convert into a modified endowment contract by the IRS, which can create tax liabilities, meaning that you would owe tax on withdrawing cash value.

According to a 2023 Nerdwallet article, the types of life insurance policies that you can use to invest your cash are whole life insurance or universal life insurance policies.

Whole Life Insurance

Whole life insurance policies are pretty straightforward. They have fixed premiums (the amount you pay per month) and permanent, guaranteed death benefits to your designated beneficiaries. This means that when you die, the beneficiary listed will receive a payout equivalent to the policy value. Your cash value will grow at a fixed rate set by your policy, meaning it won't fluctuate with the market.

Universal Life Insurance

Universal life insurance is more flexible and can grow more, but the death benefit, premiums, and cash value are not guaranteed. They may change with the market, making this a slightly riskier way to grow cash value. On the other hand, you can increase or decrease premiums and death benefits within certain parameters if you realize you want to pay more or you need to reduce them.

Variable Universal Life Insurance

Variable universal life insurance is a type of universal life insurance that allows you to adjust your premiums and death benefits while also giving you control over how to invest any cash value through subaccounts. Cash value grows based on the sub account options and their performance on the market, or the insurance policy may offer a fixed interest rate based on the policy.

Indexed Universal Life Insurance

As another type of universal life insurance, indexed universal life insurance gives similar flexibility in the types of coverage and values. However, cash value earns interest differently with these policies. In this case, the growth is based on how the stock indexes perform. It's kind of like investing in the stock market, so during good market conditions, the cash value grows quicker.

Unlike the stock market, however, an indexed universal life policy typically has an interest floor, meaning cash value will never grow less than a set amount, which is often 0%. What that means is that when the stock market crashes, your cash value is protected. This also comes with interest caps, meaning that your cash value can never accrue interest at a higher rate than whatever is set, even if the stock market sees better performance.

Other types of life insurance exist as well, but these are the main ones used for their cash value. Make sure that you speak with your insurance agent before making any decisions. They will be able to help you understand the terms, answer questions you may have, and recommend the right kinds of coverage for you.

Investments and Retirement Accounts

Investing money is risky and isn't guaranteed, but it is commonly used to grow cash value. By investing smartly, you can increase your chances of seeing growth in your money. Some are tax-advantaged, meaning that they help save you money that would otherwise be spent on taxes or allow you to invest pre-tax income into them, lowering your overall tax obligation.

Types of Investment Accounts

Investing your money will help it grow, and there are plenty of options that you can choose from. Financial planners, brokers, and investment advisors can help you review your options and help you make the best decisions for you and your unique situation.

- ✧ **Annuities:** These are insurance products you can use to create regular income during retirement. Some can be tax-deferred.

- ✧ **Mutual funds:** Mutual funds are managed by a professional who pools together bonds, stocks, and other investments that then get divided into shares and sold to people who want to invest.

- ✧ **Stocks:** Stocks represent a share of ownership in a specific corporation. Their value rises and falls based on the performance of the market or the specific company.

- ✧ **Bonds:** When investing in bonds, you pay to loan money to an issuer, like the government or a business, and you receive interest payments on top of the face value.

- ✧ **ETFs:** An exchange-traded fund (ETF) is an investment that trades like a stock on an exchange but may also include sector indexes or collections of assets.

- ✧ **Dividend reinvestment plans:** DRIPs let you reinvest your cash dividends into more stock instead of receiving cash dividends.

- ✧ **Cash investments:** Certificates of deposits (CDs) and money market deposit accounts allow you to invest income short-term in low-risk settings while allowing you to receive interest.

Types of Retirement Accounts

Retirement accounts allow you to invest your income to use specifically for retirement. They can be used effectively, but there are often penalties if you try to withdraw income early. These are the most common ones you'll encounter:

- ✧ **Defined benefit plans:** Also referred to as pensions, these plans are funded by employers, guaranteeing specific benefits based on how much you made and how long you worked with a company. However, they're not very common if you don't work for the public sector.

- ✧ **401(k)s:** 401(k)s are sponsored by employers that employees pay into. The money is usually taken out of your pay automatically and then invested, and sometimes even matched up to a certain amount each year.

- ✧ **Traditional IRAs:** IRAs are retirement accounts that allow you to defer taxes on your contributions. This allows you to invest more upfront because you can put what would have gone to taxes toward the account. Then, when you withdraw the money in retirement, you're taxed at your income rate.

✧ **Roth IRAs:** Unlike traditional IRAs, Roth IRAs are not tax deductible. However, other than that, they work the same as a traditional IRA (Folger, 2022).

Especially if you have an offer from an employer to match your contributions into these retirement accounts, you should try to max them out each year as often as possible to get the most out of them.

Chapter Summary

Investing now will set you up in the future. The sooner you start, the more your money can grow into what you will eventually need. It's never too soon to start thinking about retirement, and when you free yourself from financial stress, you can start thinking about other things, like your relationships.

PART 3

RELATIONSHIPS AND COMMUNICATION

> *Communication to a relationship is like oxygen is to life. Without it, it dies.*
>
> *–Tony A. Gaskins Jr.*

CHAPTER 8

DIFFERENT RELATIONSHIPS, SAME FOUNDATIONS

We all crave relationships in our lives. Friendships, familial relationships, romantic partners, and even workplace relationships help meet our social needs and can make us feel fulfilled and confident in ourselves. I don't know where I'd be in life without my family or friends, and I'm sure you feel the same way.

But relationships aren't easy to maintain, and knowing how to spot and leave a bad relationship can be even harder. Knowing how to navigate relationships is one of the most important skills you can learn. Part of being able to navigate is knowing how to communicate, which we'll discuss in the next chapter. Part of it is also knowing what goes into fostering and maintaining those connections. After all, they're two-way streets.

No matter what kind of relationship you're talking about, they all should be based on mutual trust, honesty, open communication, and respect. Remember that you deserve to be treated well, and respect is a basic human decency, not something that needs to be earned.

Relationships should make you feel good. They should make you feel heard and seen, and you should feel like you can be yourself in them. Those that don't make you feel good or those that show signs of red flags can be harmful to your mental health. I've had toxic friendships and I know how much they can mess with your mind. I know what it's like to feel like I was the problem and that if I changed, I could enjoy the relationship that I wanted with the other person. The truth was, the foundation for a healthy relationship just wasn't there with them.

The Foundation of a Healthy Relationship

Relationships of all kinds are hard work. Yes, it seems like this is something that should be simple, but the reality is they aren't. They take a lot of effort to maintain, but in the end, the effort is worth it. There will be times that you fight with those you care about, and we'll talk about solving those conflicts in a healthy manner in the next chapter. No matter what is going on in your relationship, however, these four factors should be present. You should always feel like there is a foundation of honesty, trust, open communication, and respect, even in conflicts.

Honesty

Honesty is where transparency and authenticity shine through. It is what allows you to tell the other person anything without fear of judgment or backlash and what allows the other person to come to you as well. It's easy to feel tempted to slip into dishonesty to avoid hurting someone's feelings, but this isn't a good way to approach the situation. It can be harmful to the relationship because you aren't being straightforward.

Honesty involves being able to share what you feel and trust the other person with that information, building intimacy. Intimacy isn't limited to just romantic relationships, either. To be intimate with someone is to be *close* to them. It's to be connected and supported and comfortable with the other person, and it's present in most personal relationships to various degrees. Yes, you're usually the most intimate with your romantic partner if you have one, but sharing your thoughts and secrets with your best friend or a parent is another way to be intimate.

Trust

Trust in relationships allows you to feel safe and confident with the other person. You know that they will not hurt or betray you. As a result, you can be vulnerable and honest with that other person. Friends, family members, and romantic partners can all be some of our most valued confidantes, allowing us to connect and show our truest selves to them.

Trust brings so much to our relationships. It fosters positivity, forgiveness, and closeness. It helps us to navigate and reduce conflict because when you trust someone, you feel more compelled to find solutions and common ground or to give them the benefit of the doubt when (not if!) they mess up.

Trust is a beautiful thing, but it's also something that has to be built and fostered. It's fragile and easy to destroy, and once you damage trust, rebuilding it is even harder. To foster it, you need to communicate honestly and be on the same page with the other person.

Without trust, you can harm your relationship, eroding it with secrecy and pushing away your loved one. Trust can be hurt by insecurity, which can make you even more insecure in your relationship with the other person.

Open Communication

Open communication builds upon the previous two foundations, helping to secure the relationship by discussing anything that may get in the way of it. Problems and fights happen. In fact, according to John Gottman, a relationship researcher, the magic ratio between positive and negative interactions is 5:1, meaning that for every one negative interaction, there should be five positive ones. That sounds like a lot more negative interactions between people than would be expected, but it just goes to show how common conflict really is.

That's why it's so important to have open communication. Not only will it build trust in a relationship, but it will also help solve those conflicts in a constructive manner, which will help you to strengthen your connection with the other person.

Respect

The problem with respect is that so many people see it differently. You've got a whole group of people who believe that respecting someone is listening to them, while other people say respect is treating someone with basic human decency. The respect you need in any relationship is the kind where you regard them with kindness. You treat them well like you'd want to be treated.

Mutual respect forms the foundation of relationships of all kinds and is shown through giving consideration to the other person's feelings, thoughts, and boundaries. To respect someone is to show you care about them through how you act and speak toward them. It can also involve being accountable for your actions when you make a mistake or hurt someone's feelings. No relationship is perfect, but respecting the other person should be a common pattern.

Relationship Red Flags

Red flags can pop up in just about any relationship, from romantic partners to coworkers. When you see red flags waving, it's your sign to run like the wind, or at least consider the relationship heavily because there's something toxic going on. Some of these red flags may not be obvious if you're not looking for them, but they are a sign that the other person isn't likely to be in a healthy relationship of any kind.

Violent Or Abusive Actions

While violence is straightforward, abuse can take several different forms, all of which are red flags. You can experience abuse in more than just romantic relationships too. Friends, family, and coworkers can be abusive. Some types of abuse include:

- ✧ **Physical abuse:** This is any type of physical violence or threats used to keep control of a situation. It includes throwing, breaking, or destroying objects.

- ✧ **Emotional abuse:** Emotional abuse is a lot harder to identify because it's non-physical. It's any behavior designed to isolate, control, or scare you, like name-calling, insults, possessiveness, trying to get you to cut off your friends or family, monitoring your behaviors, humiliating you in front of others, gaslighting, and blaming you for their abusive actions. It could also include threatening you or damaging your belongings.

- ✧ **Financial abuse:** When a partner limits access to finances or actively hinders your ability to earn money, they are financially abusive. This isn't the same as expecting adherence to a budget—it involves actively preventing access to funds, maxing out your credit cards, a refusal to contribute while expecting you to work for everything, or refusing money for necessary expenses.

- ✧ **Sexual abuse:** Sexual abuse happens when a partner or other person takes control of physical and sexual intimacy without consent. It includes manipulating or guilting into having sex, nonconsensual sexual actions, ignoring how you feel about sex, or intentionally attempting to give you a sexually transmitted infection. Sexual abuse can be present in any kind of relationship or even without a relationship with the other person.

✧ **Digital abuse:** Digital abuse uses the internet to bully, intimidate, or control a partner, often through emotional abuse.

✧ **Stalking:** Stalkers follow, harass, or watch their target despite being told to stop, causing them to feel uncomfortable, unsafe, or afraid.

Mismatch in Goals

This is more of a romantic relationship red flag than any other kind. When you and your partner want vastly different things, it's a red flag for the relationship because it means someone will have to give up their wants for the other party. For example, if you want children but your romantic partner doesn't, you have to grapple with whether you're willing to forego having kids to keep your partner or if you're both simply too incompatible for each other. It could also involve career goals, how to handle finances, or irreconcilable political or religious differences.

Jealousy

When someone is constantly jealous when you spend time with other people, regardless of what your relationship with them is, it's a sign of insecurity. That insecurity can be incredibly damaging to your relationship and cause issues down the road. It can also be a sign of possessiveness.

Lack of Trust

Trust is the foundation of all relationships, and without it, there's no real healthy relationship.

Lying or Infidelity

Both lying and infidelity involve dishonest behaviors and can be major red flags in any relationship. People comfortable with lying to you often continue to lie, and without being able to trust the other person, it's hard to maintain any kind of relationship.

Controlling

People who attempt to control you by limiting access to other people, telling you what to do, or otherwise attempting to monitor your behavior are usually not respectful of your autonomy. While, especially at work, there's some expectation that your supervisors will tell you what to do, it shouldn't get to the point where it's controlling you outside of work as well.

Stories of "Crazy Exes"

This goes for friends, bosses, coworkers, and romantic partners. If the person you are speaking to has a bunch of stories about how other people are all problematic for a bunch of reasons, there's a good chance that you're not getting the whole picture. For example, if your new romantic partner has a whole slew of exes that all are terrible, dishonest, and controlling, there's a chance that your partner actually has unresolved issues that will make it difficult to have a meaningful, healthy relationship with them and they perceive healthy boundaries, conversations, and expectations as wrong.

Inability to Maintain Friendships

People who have no friends or struggle to maintain friends or relationships often have a reason for it. This is especially true if you hear a lot of deflection and refusal to take personal accountability for any part in their situation.

Gaslighting

Gaslighting can be a huge problem in many relationships, causing you to think that you are wrong. It happens when someone says or does things that make you question your own perception of what happened. For example, they might say they don't know what you did with your phone when you notice that it's not on the counter anymore and mention how you often lose it when, in fact, they have it in their pocket. They can use other tactics to manipulate you and make you feel like you're the problem instead in an attempt to control you and your behavior.

Love Bombing

Love bombing is the attempt to gain love and trust quickly by showering someone with praise and affection. They may tell you how much they love you, how you're different from everyone they've ever known, or give you plenty of gifts in an attempt to make you feel good. By making you feel good, adored, and desired, they essentially create an addiction to those feelings, but it usually fades over time. Once you're hooked, you get less affection and adoration, so you chase after getting back to that pedestal, which is how the person love bombing gets control.

Breadcrumbing

Breadcrumbing is another way to play with your feelings by giving you just enough affection or encouragement to keep you hooked on the relationship. However, as you try to get closer, they'll pull back. If you start to lose interest, they'll give you more. There's no commitment with this type of hot-and-cold behavior.

Chapter Summary

While you're not defined by the people around you, they do influence you. Healthy relationships of all kinds need healthy foundations, and as you gain more experience in life, you'll learn to spot the red flags and know when something isn't quite right. This will help you to communicate better in your relationships, too, because you'll be able to articulate what you see that's wrong and make moves to fix the problems. The next chapter is all about learning healthy, effective communication techniques.

CHAPTER 9

DEVELOPING HEALTHY COMMUNICATION SKILLS

Communication can be *hard.* You can say one thing and the other person can hear something completely different from what you intended to convey. Back when I was dating my husband, I remember a conversation we had when we just weren't on the same page. We had an argument that was so unimportant I can't even remember what it was about. I just remember feeling frustrated, unheard, and unloved. We weren't on the same page, and I really thought it'd be the end of our relationship.

Nowadays, we have much better skills regarding our communication. We're capable of talking through our issues and finding common ground that will help us to get past our conflicts. Don't get me wrong, those arguments still suck. It's never fun to fight with someone you care about, but it's much easier to get back on the same page and keep moving forward when you have the right tools in your toolbox.

Communicating Effectively

The best thing you can do for your relationships of all kinds is learn how to communicate clearly and effectively. These are strategies that I've implemented and dedicated myself to teaching my own children to better prepare them for adulthood and I think that anyone could benefit from them. If you put these tools to the test, especially if your loved ones do them with you (remember, communication is a two-way street, after all!), then you'll probably see improvements in how you interact and get along with each other too. It all begins with learning how to listen actively, and then begin putting these strategies to good use.

Active Listening

When you listen actively, you do more than just hear the words the other person has to say. It's about really understanding the meaning of the words being told to you before you ever begin formatting a response. All too often, people get so caught up in trying to respond as quickly as they can or thinking of how they'll respond instead of paying attention to what's being conveyed.

To listen actively, you need to:

✧ Be present in the conversation, giving it your complete focus.

✧ Hold eye contact and open body language to convey interest in the conversation.

✧ Pay attention to body language cues.

✧ Instead of responding, ask open-ended questions to encourage the other person to elaborate.

✧ Before responding, paraphrase what you have heard to make sure that you're both on the same page.

✧ Listen without judgment or without giving advice unless it's asked for.

How to Communicate Effectively

Being able to listen only helps with half of the communication. After all, it takes two to communicate; otherwise, it's just a lecture. Communicating effectively requires you to be comfortable with not only listening but also with responding.

Choosing to speak concisely is a great way to help improve communication skills. Stick to the basics, especially when emotions run high. I've experienced arguments that quickly devolve because we get stuck on tangents instead of focusing on what matters the most, and it's never fun. To avoid this, if you have to have a heavy conversation, try planning it ahead of time.

While sometimes, these conversations pop up when you least expect them, there's nothing wrong with stopping in the moment, saying you need some time to think, and coming back to the conversation when you and the other person are calmer and able to tackle it on with a level-headed approach. Some other great ways to keep your communication clear include:

✧ **Pay attention to body language:** Your body speaks just as much as your mouth does, and if you're not careful, you may send off cues that disrupt what you actually want to say. For example, if your body language comes off as angry, the other person may get defensive, which will shut down any effective communication.

✧ **Be careful with your tone:** Like body language, how you speak and your tone of voice will also influence what you're trying to say. Would you want to listen to someone tell you how to be confident if they stuttered and stumbled over their words in the most timid voice you've ever heard? Probably not! Speak calmly, especially during important conversations.

✧ **Avoid judgment:** You don't necessarily have to agree with what the other person has to say, but you should hold off on judgment. When you communicate with someone, you need to be open to what they have to say and hear them out to truly understand what they're saying.

✧ **Pause before you speak:** This goes back to taking the time to communicate clearly. While you don't necessarily have to take a break mid-conversation, you should take a moment to breathe before responding to make sure you've thought out what you want to say.

✧ **Use "I" statements:** Especially when emotions are high, you should stick to "I" statements. For example, "I feel like you don't have time for me" is a much more effective phrase compared to "You never make time for me." Instead of making it an attack or a judgment, you're discussing your feelings instead.

This stops defensiveness or arguing over whether that's actually the case or just your perspective on it (which is valid, too!).

By learning to communicate better, you can help avoid conflicts, but not all of them can be dodged. It's only natural for there to be disagreements sometimes, and that's okay! You and the other person, no matter who they are to you, don't have to see eye to eye on every single thing. You're both unique people with your own thoughts, feelings, and experiences guiding you.

Conflict Resolution

As natural as conflict is in every relationship, it's still a big drag, and it can be something that a lot of us try to run away from. Running from conflicts and constantly people-pleasing to avoid them can both be huge detriments to your relationships and your mental health. As tempting as it can be to ignore them, all this does is let them continue to fester and worsen, and when they finally explode, the results can be disastrous. But conflicts are also opportunities for growth and bettering your relationships with other people. They let you build trust and feel secure that you and the other person can work through your disagreements.

Because conflict triggers such strong emotions that can get the best of us sometimes, it's important to stay ahead of your stress level when you face one. To handle a conflict healthily, sometimes you need to put a pin in it for later to calm down, which is absolutely valid, as long as you come back to it later instead of ignoring it.

Solving your conflicts will require you to:

- ✧ manage your stress without getting distracted.
- ✧ stay grounded and control your behavior while managing your emotions.
- ✧ listen to the other person's feelings.
- ✧ respect your differences.

Sounds easy enough, right? Well, like all things worth doing well, it's easier said than done. Try implementing some of these strategies to help defuse your conflicts.

No Interruptions

Take turns speaking instead of constantly trying to butt in. Let one person have the floor to speak their mind while the other listens actively. Once you confirm you understand what the other person is saying, you can formulate your response.

Discuss From a Place of Curiosity

A lot of times, conflicts arise because you and the other person aren't on the same page. Approaching the conversation from a place of curiosity and without judgment allows both of you to better understand each other. You may learn something new about the other person, which can be useful in avoiding future conflicts over the same issue.

Use Repair Attempts

Repair attempts are ways that we try to reconnect with someone after a conflict arises. They can help assure the other person that you see that there's a problem and that you want to de-escalate. Some people turn to humor (but make sure the other person won't get more upset!), say you understand, and show positive, open body language. You could even offer a hug or hold their hand to show that you care and don't want to continue fighting.

Apologize—The Right Way

Genuine apologies are more than just saying, "I'm sorry." They should also say what you did wrong, why it was wrong, and what you'll do in the future to avoid the problem. They should also include some sort of restitution—an offer to make it right. Apologies should never be followed by "but" or other words that immediately imply you're going to deflect or justify your actions.

For example, "I'm sorry I broke your laptop. I really wasn't paying attention to where I was walking, and I didn't mean to knock it off the desk. I'll be sure to pay more attention in the future to avoid this. Is there anything I can do to make it up to you?"

Ask What They Need

This is a point that should go both ways. You should tell the other person what you need while also asking them what they need to find some sort of resolution. Don't be afraid to vocalize what you need from them to prevent this from being an issue again in the future. They aren't mind readers, and neither are you. This helps boost communication and keep you both on the same page.

Find a Compromise

In many conflicts, a compromise can be a great way to put an end to the argument. While it's not always right (or fair) to expect a compromise, such as if you have a roommate who never cleans up after themselves (been there, done that!) and you're sick of playing maid, in many cases, compromise can be one of your most valuable tools.

For example, imagine that you and your best friend both have vastly different ideas for a fun night. Your friend wants to go out to the club or hang out at a party while you prefer staying in. A valid compromise is that you go out one night and stay in the next. Or, let's say you like to sleep with a TV on but your college dorm roommate prefers to sleep in the dark and silence. A good compromise here could be you watching videos on your phone with the screen dimmed and a set of headphones so you both mostly get what you want.

Sometimes, compromises may seem unreasonable to you, especially if they push you past certain boundaries that you have. It's okay, and even healthy, to have boundaries, and that means you also need to know how to enforce them.

Boundary Setting

Boundaries are the lines you draw in relationships that you do not tolerate being crossed. It could be something like don't take food off your plate or that you want to be called a certain name. Your boundaries are a form of self-care that help you to feel safe and secure in your relationship. They should be communicated clearly and protected as long as they're healthy.

Unhealthy boundaries can be dangerous and tend to either harm or hold you back or attempt to exert control over someone else. Some common unhealthy boundaries (which are also red flags in relationships!) are:

✧ putting yourself down or letting someone else put you down.

✧ attempts to control someone else's behavior, such as saying that the other person can't have any friends other than you.

✧ attempts to change someone else, telling them how to act or what to do.

The boundaries you'll enforce in your life will be related to you and your wishes. Healthy ones create a sort of reflection of your lifestyle, showcasing the rules, principles, and guidelines that you have for your relationships. Some common healthy boundaries you may choose include:

✧ refusing to be manipulated or blamed for someone else's actions.

✧ expecting to be treated with respect and kindness.

✧ asking for space when you need it and expecting the request to be respected.

✧ communicating what makes you uncomfortable and expecting the request to be respected.

✧ expecting a certain degree of privacy with journals, passwords, or certain feelings or events.

✧ expecting your time to be respected.

✧ expressing sexual boundaries and expecting them to be respected.

✧ expecting your religion (or lack thereof) to be respected.

✧ protecting your material possessions and what will and won't be shared.

Your exact boundaries may deviate from these, such as saying that if someone leaves you hanging and doesn't respect your time, then you'll stop waiting for them. It's okay to protect your boundaries, and although it might feel like you're retaliating against the person who broke them, you aren't. If your boundaries are broken, especially repeatedly and after many attempts at communicating them clearly, then you are well within your rights to remove yourself from the situation.

Setting Your Boundaries

Establishing your boundaries shouldn't be difficult in a healthy relationship, especially if you put your good communication skills to the test. It's all about communicating them and it's often best to do so in a moment of calmness. After a boundary has been crossed, handle the natural anger you feel first and then write down what's bothering you so you won't forget it.

When you've calmed down, you can go to the other person and calmly and clearly state what happened and how it made you feel. You can then assert your boundary, stating exactly what that boundary is, that you will not tolerate it being crossed or ignored, and why it's a problem.

This should come from a place of love and kindness, explaining that you trust the other person not to violate your boundaries, and you should follow up by asking the other person if there are any boundaries that they need enforcing. They should have some things that they state are their non-negotiable points. You can model good boundary respecting as well by following theirs and apologizing whenever you make a mistake.

Setting and enforcing your boundaries is part of keeping yourself healthy. Your mental health and self-care are just as important as feeding yourself or sleeping. Remember that your boundaries are what allow you to feel safe and secure, and in healthy relationships of all kinds, people respect those boundaries.

Chapter Summary

Healthy communication will take you far in life. It'll help you to relate to others, express your own boundaries, and solve conflicts. Skills like active listening and learning not to interrupt others can all help you to be more successful in your communication, and when you can communicate well, you can work better with the people that surround you, whether they're coworkers, classmates, or your friends and family, reducing stress, and increasing positive feelings. All of this can have an overall impact on your general health too.

Moving into the next section of the book, we're taking a closer look at your physical and mental health, which go hand in hand.

PART 4

HEALTH AND WELLNESS

Self-care is not selfish. You cannot serve from an empty vessel.

–Eleanor Brown

CHAPTER 10

PHYSICAL AND MENTAL HEALTH GO HAND-IN-HAND

Your body and mind might seem like two separate things, but the truth is, they're more connected than most people would think. From the gut-brain axis influencing the neurotransmitters that make you think and feel to exercise being a fantastic way to boost energy levels and mental health, the two are highly linked. The best way to take care of your mind is to take care of your body and vice versa. After all, how good will you feel mentally if your body aches or is too tired to do anything? Or how good do you think you'd feel physically if you're stuck in anxiety or depression?

By taking care of both your body and mind, you'll feel your best. That means getting enough sleep, eating healthily, and keeping hydrated. It also means being able to guard your mental health with healthy boundaries and good mindsets. When both your body and mind are healthy, you have more energy and mental bandwidth to take care of the things you need to do, like work, keep stress levels down, or maintain good relationships.

The Connection Between Physical and Mental Health

Our bodies react to our perceptions of the world around us that our minds generate. When you think something is scary, your body responds in kind, entering the fight, flight, or freeze response. While your college final is a far stretch from being as dangerous as a lion staring you down, your body still reacts the same way to stress-inducing events, regardless of the actual threat level they may pose.

Now, imagine that you constantly live with stress. You're busy with school and work, and you want to spend time with friends. Or you're having a hard time somewhere. What do you think your body does? Those stress hormones prepare your body to fend off the potential threat, causing your heart to race, inducing anxiety, and building up cortisol. This redirects your body's energy and efforts to survival instead of maintenance processes that usually happen at rest.

While short bursts of these hormones aren't a big deal for your body; when you live under a constant state of stress, cortisol, a stress hormone, can cause inflammation throughout your body. Extended periods of exposure to this can lead to depression and constant feelings of fatigue while also weakening your immune system. In other words, people who are stressed often get or feel sick, and it can also increase their risk of several diseases.

Much of what you need to do to stay healthy uses this connection between body and mind. Exercise, for example, is great for you and boosts your mood. Eating healthy foods encourages a healthy gut biome, which also leads to having more energy and feeling better overall.

Maintaining a Healthy Body and Mind

Your body is the only one you get, so taking care of it is important. Yeah, you're young and your body can bounce back from a lot more than mine can. You can probably eat that extra slice of pizza without a care in the world, whereas I have indigestion if I so much as think about indulging. Just because you're young doesn't mean that you should neglect your health, even if your body can take it.

When I was in college, I lived off cheap ramen, pizza, and microwave meals. Let me tell you, if I tried to make that my diet today, it wouldn't be a fun time. I also rarely bothered with exercise and lived by the motto of "Sleep is for the weak! I'll sleep when I'm dead." It's a wonder my body never gave out on me from the years of abuse in my young adult years.

Nowadays, I make sure I walk the dogs for at least an hour most days. I eat healthy, well-balanced meals. I'm that boring old lady that goes to sleep at 10 each night when before, I'd still be getting ready for that night out. And you know what? My body feels so much better for it. I've noticed the slip in my mood and energy levels when I'm not taking care of myself the way I should be.

Taking care of yourself might feel like a huge time sink, but like saving for the future, it's an investment in yourself and your long-term health.

Sleep

While teens need an average of 8–10 hours of sleep per day, including potential naps, adults need around 7. I know, I know. If you're in college and have a job and a semi-healthy social life, it's more likely that you'll live off of copious amounts of coffee, energy drinks, and the occasional quick nap between classes in the library. Here in Seattle, I've walked through the campus at the University of Washington to enjoy the cherry blossom blooming and have seen students sleeping in the grass under the trees!

When we're busy, it's easy to make sleep the first thing we cut, but your body needs it consistently. Getting those 7 hours of sleep each day should be a major priority for you whenever possible. This is best done by consistently sleeping and waking at the same time. Of course, young adults have lives to live and people to see, but your sleep quality will have a major impact on your overall health and well-being.

Try keeping your room dark, comfortable, and relaxing. If you're able to, avoid electronics from the bedroom and try to skip large meals, caffeine, or alcohol before bed. All of this helps foster healthier sleep, which can leave you feeling better overall. Exercise can also help you sleep easier at night.

Exercise

Exercise helps you to maintain a healthy weight, but it also does more than that. It can improve your mood, brain health and keep you energetic, as well as strengthen your body and reduce the risk of many diseases. Ideally, you'd be active at least 150 minutes per week, which sounds like a lot but it is really just 30 minutes five days per week. Part of getting your exercise in for the day should include two days of strength training, making sure to focus on all major muscle groups at least once.

If this is tough to schedule in, there are plenty of ways to change up your daily schedule to stay active and still reap the benefits. Try implementing some of these:

✧ If you work at a desk often, use a standing desk.

✧ Walk to work, class, or on errands instead of driving if possible.

✧ Park in the back of parking lots and walk inside instead of parking as close to the store as possible.

✧ Take the stairs instead of the elevators.

✧ Implement a daily walk after work to decompress.

✧ Wake up 30 minutes early to get a quick workout in from home.

✧ Use an under-desk bicycle for some extra exercise.

✧ When you're watching TV, get a quick bit of exercise in during commercials.

✧ Have some basic small exercise equipment at home or easily available for at-home workouts.

✧ Use the weekend to catch up on missed exercise during the work or school week.

The more consistently you exercise, the easier it will become, and soon, you may find that you feel much better than you did before.

Diet

Eating healthily can be a challenge. From healthy whole foods often being more expensive than processed foods to needing to find time to meal plan and prep, it can be tough to squeeze it in. We've already addressed plenty of ways to implement a good, healthy meal plan, but now's the time to dive into what makes a healthy meal and how it'll benefit you.

Eating healthy meals can improve overall wellness by providing everything your body needs to thrive. It's associated with benefits such as longer lives, healthy skin, teeth, and eyes, and a lower risk of heart disease, type 2 diabetes, and cancer. It's also a major component in maintaining a healthy weight.

On the mental health frontier, a healthy diet full of nutrient-rich foods decreases mood swings and improves your ability to focus for longer periods. Some studies also suggest that clean diets can improve the symptoms of depression and anxiety, as opposed to unhealthy diets being associated with an increased risk of dementia or stroke.

Healthy diets often are fiber-rich, which helps keep your blood sugar (and energy) steady to avoid sugar crashes. Antioxidants in healthy foods fight inflammation, which can help counteract the effect of long-term stress. Probiotic-rich fermented foods improve your gut bacteria biome, which can leave you feeling better as well. Folate, a B vitamin, manages dopamine production, while vitamin D, which you get from sunlight and foods like mushrooms, can boost serotonin and moods. Magnesium is crucial for nerve and muscle function while also keeping your gut bacteria healthy. Mineral deficiencies can set your biome off-kilter, which can lead to anxiety and depression symptoms.

Implementing a wide range of whole foods is one of the easiest ways to get everything your body needs. It can be tempting to just pop multivitamin supplements, but keep in mind that the nutrients in food are often much more bioavailable than in supplement form, meaning that your body can better benefit from them in food sources.

I know how hard it is to get a rainbow on your plate every day, a way that many people rely on to get a range of vitamins in their diet. However, there are little changes you can make that will taste great and help keep your body healthy. This is what I do to make sure I get most of what I need in my diet.

Add More Fiber

Fiber keeps you full and your blood sugar stable. I keep prepped veggies available in my fridge to grab whenever I need a quick snack. Celery and carrots do great in jars of water! They last much longer than if you just left them in a bag. Reach for whole grains, beans, and lentils when you really need some staying power in your diet.

Vitamin D and Calcium Go Hand in Hand

When eaten together, vitamin D and calcium have a synergizing effect. Many foods are fortified with these nutrients to boost their bioavailability. Foods like milk, salmon, and dark, leafy greens will give you the boost you need. Remember, we get a lot of our vitamin D from sunlight, so don't forget to get outdoors!

Skip the Added Sugars

Added sugar may taste good, but all it does is prepare you for some serious sugar crashes. Instead of soda, opt for water with fruit slices, or use fresh fruit to sweeten your yogurt instead of buying the sweetened stuff.

Healthy Fats

We need fats to function, but only if they're the right kind. Ditch the saturated fats for unsaturated ones, like olive oil, instead of canola oil or margarine. Limit red meats in favor of seafood or vegetarian meals, and when you do choose pork or beef, try to choose leaner cuts.

Be Careful With Salts

We need both salt and potassium in balance with each other for our nerves to work. However, it's really easy to get too much salt and not enough potassium, which can leave you feeling unwell and raise your blood pressure. Cut out food from restaurants and processed sources and make your own food and rely on herbs and seasonings instead of salt.

An ideal plate will be half fruits and veggies (ideally of different colors), a quarter whole grains, and a quarter protein. Especially if you live in the United States, you probably have the idea that your meal is built around protein, but really, it should be built around the plant-based foods you choose.

Food is expensive, but it's also an important way to keep your body healthy. It's another way of self-care. Another way to look at it is that if you eat healthy foods, you may save money on medical expenses.

Chapter Summary

Your health is one of the biggest investments you'll ever make in yourself. Yes, it can be expensive to take care of yourself well with rising food costs, but this is one where you shouldn't skimp if you don't have to. You can still be mindful of expenses and eat well if you put together good meal plans and keep a healthy diet, and having a healthy body is one of the best ways to make sure that you have a healthy mind as well. In the next chapter, we're going to discuss just how important self-care is and what you need to do to keep your mental health in good shape.

CHAPTER 11

SELF-CARE AND HEALTHY HABITS

Skipping out on self-care is another thing we tend to do to maintain our busy schedules. Why take that mental health time when you have to study and write that paper or you have overtime for the week and still have chores to do? Well, the answer is simple: You can't be on the go constantly and worrying about everything but yourself. Taking time to implement self-care can be one of the best ways to avoid burnout and improve your mental health. Some aspects of self-care are meeting your basic physical needs, like we talked about in the last chapter. Eating good foods, sleeping well, and keeping your body in shape with exercise are all forms of self-care.

I've been hit by burnout before, exhausted and feeling like I didn't have the mental energy to do *anything*. I didn't want to do chores and they piled up. I could barely drag myself out of bed to work or get to class. I had chosen a particularly heavy course load for the quarter and was maxing out the number of credits I could take as a full-time student. I also worked to pay my bills and support myself at the time. I was up at 6 a.m. to get ready for school, had classes from 8–3 most days, with small breaks between them that I spent working on homework and studying. I worked from 6–10 p.m. most days, got home at 10:30 p.m., and did homework til close to 2–3 a.m. most days. I threw out exercise, time with friends, and my hobbies, telling myself it was temporary and I'd be fine.

Halfway through the quarter, midterms came around, and I had two long research papers and two exams to study for, plus my usual work. Of course, most of my coworkers were also college students and had asked for extra time off, which led to me being scheduled for longer shifts than usual. I was eating nothing but processed garbage when I could spare a few minutes and awake through the magic of caffeine.

One evening, on my way to work, I found myself feeling completely drained. I drank another energy drink and went on my way, only to start feeling jittery and lightheaded, like I'd pass out if I didn't sit down. Long story short, I got sent home from work by my manager because he was afraid I'd genuinely pass out at work and had the longest sleep I had for weeks.

My dear husband, who was my long-term boyfriend at the time, fussed over me and babied me for the rest of the evening, giving me that "I told you so" look without actually saying the words out loud. And sure enough, he *had* told me so. He'd tried to discourage me from taking so many classes or accepting so many hours. He'd encouraged me to ask for time off that week well in advance, but I was convinced we needed the money. He'd begged me to take time to myself to rest and relax when he'd catch me dozing off on my textbooks at my desk, but I told him I couldn't. Long story short, he was right. He loved me and wanted me to take care of myself. I had assumed that I'd have time to rest later.

Why Self-Care Matters

Self-care matters because it keeps us from burning out, it relieves the pressures of daily life, and lets us rest. Without rest, it's hard to maintain high levels of productivity for long. You might get a quick burst out of foregoing the self-care, but it's not sustainable, and you can very quickly end up like me, exhausted and feeling like utter garbage. I burnt the proverbial candle from both ends and by the time it was completely gone, I was in need of some serious rest.

I could have completely avoided the problem with self-care, which is proven to reduce anxiety, depression, and stress. As a result, it makes us more able to concentrate, feel happier, and have more energy. Speaking purely physically, self-care has been shown to reduce heart disease, cancer, and stroke. It can also greatly improve our quality of life by encouraging us to follow our passions and remain rooted in what we want and need the most in life.

Types of Self-Care

Self-care can take many different forms, from taking care of our bodies to finding things we love to do and making time for them. I like to break down self-care into three categories, depending on what it does for us at the time: physical, emotional, and spiritual.

Physical Self-Care

Physical self-care is all about taking care of your body and involves most of what we talked about in the previous chapter.

Emotional Self-Care

Emotional self-care emphasizes how we take care of our mental health. It can involve our self-talk, setting boundaries to protect us from unnecessary stress, or taking time to ourselves to rest and enjoy ourselves. Try setting up a coffee date with a friend or a weekly movie or game night that you can count on to unwind. Remember, you have permission to unwind and rest. Protect that. You work to live, you don't live to work, and that's a lesson I learned far too late in life.

Emotional self-care comes in several forms, with my favorites being:

✧ accepting and allowing yourself to feel what you feel

✧ learning your emotional triggers and how to work with them

✧ putting your needs first and tending to them

✧ maintaining your boundaries

✧ avoiding negative people and places

✧ using self-compassion and not being too hard on yourself

✧ asking for help when you need it

✧ resting when you need it

✧ finding time each day to do something you love

Spiritual Self-Care

Spiritual self-care is very personal. For some, it's focusing on their religion. For others, it's finding ways to care for themselves deeply through meditation or regular acts of kindness, or a gratitude journal. It's all about developing a deeper sense of meaning within yourself, fostering and nurturing a sense of your beliefs and values. Some ways I practice spiritual self-care include:

✧ practicing yoga

✧ meditating

✧ finding ways to connect to the greater community, such as joining clubs or volunteering

✧ taking time to get into nature

✧ practicing forgiveness and letting go of grudges or negative emotions

Starting a Self-Care Routine

Building a self-care routine can be tough if you've gotten into the habit of putting your needs last or ignoring them. It can feel selfish or like you're putting too much time into yourself when there are other things you could spend your time on. It can also be tough to get into the habit of taking the time for yourself. Making self-care your habit is one of the best ways you can support yourself. Getting into the habit can be broken down into several steps that can make it easier to implement.

Identify What Makes You Feel Centered

As much as everyone needs self-care, it also looks different for everyone. While you might think spending an hour at the gym lifting weights is a great way to spend your time, someone else might think it's brutal. Self-care is all about what you can do to feel centered and good about yourself.

Make a list of the things that you love that make you feel centered and fulfilled. Maybe you like to read and write or ride horses. Or, you could be the kind of person who loves cooking or gardening.

Think of How to Implement These Into Your Life

Once you have your list of things that help you feel centered, you need to start implementing them. Let's say your list is:

✧ listening to music

- ✧ writing
- ✧ jogging
- ✧ yoga
- ✧ spending time with friends

Now, it's time to slide those into your regular schedule. Listening to music is easy—you can pop in a pair of headphones or listen to music on your commute or while doing chores. Jogging and yoga can fit into your exercise regimen. The hard part would be fitting in writing and spending time with friends into your life, but it's important to do so. Maybe you opt to write for ten minutes before bed each night and schedule a regular weekly meetup with your friends.

Set Goals for Daily Self-Care

In two chapters, we'll be diving into how to set goals so you can achieve them, so we'll hold off on going in depth here. Setting goals to meet your self-care daily is a great way to prioritize that care, as long as you choose SMART goals. These are goals that are specific, measurable, achievable, relevant, and timely (Boogaard, 2021). Maybe you set goals to go to bed at a set time, eat a healthy diet, and get your exercise time in.

It's okay to work your goals in slowly, starting with one or two easier ones until they develop into habits. Then, you can start implementing more self-care and better address your needs.

Create a Support System

One of my favorite ways to stick to my goals, especially in self-care, is to set up a support system. This is more than just having people who cheer you on and encourage you. It's also a good idea to have people who use the same self-care activities for themselves, allowing you to both work together. If you want to exercise more to care for yourself, you can have accountability buddies that you jog or go to the gym with. Writers can write concurrently with their buddies to keep going even when they feel like writer's block is overwhelming.

Having a support system of people who self-care like you do means that you can talk together and work together to meet your goals. They'll understand your struggles and be able to talk through problems. Plus, it's always satisfying to do something with someone else and get that social interaction in too!

Take the Trial and Error Approach

The most important part about putting together your self-care routine is to remember that it's all about trial and error. What works for someone else may not work for you, and vice versa. You might also try to set up a routine that just isn't working for you. Instead of trying to browbeat yourself into being able to do it and creating negative associations, remember that it's totally valid to take a new approach.

Your needs will change over time. Your schedule will, too. That means that self-care has to be flexible to fit into your schedule. After all, you wouldn't forego a great job that overlaps with your scheduled gym time—you'd probably shift your gym time to accommodate your work schedule. Other self-care practices can be shifted around too.

Don't be afraid to mix things up if you need to find a better schedule for you. What's most important here is that you get your time for self-care and make it enjoyable.

Self-Care and Stress Relief Tips

A lot of what we've already talked about throughout the book falls into self-care. Eating well, staying hydrated, sleeping, and exercising all help your body. Setting goals and priorities can help too. There's more to self-care than just that, and many stress relief tips can also help with your practice. Here are some of my tried and true stress relief and self-care tips and tricks.

Set Up a Gratitude Journal

Gratitude journals remind you of the positives in your life and improve your mindset to be more positive. Each night before bed, I stop and write down at least three things that I'm grateful for. Even on the worst of days, there's always something I can appreciate. Some days, I've written that my husband, children, and I are alive and mostly well. Others, I've written about a sweet thing someone did for me or about the beautiful view I saw.

This helps to reframe your mindset to be something more positive just because it has you thinking about good things that happened throughout your day.

Pick Up a Self-Care Book

There are so many good books out there about self-care. We've touched upon some subjects, but this is really just an overview. Especially if you like to read, picking up a dedicated self-care book may be just what you need to get inspired and fix up your routine. They can also offer insight into areas you struggle and how to overcome them. If you're busy, you can choose an audiobook to listen to during commutes or chore time.

Enjoy a Pet Companion

Did you know that pets, particularly dogs, can reduce stress and anxiety and even lower blood pressure? There's a reason they're used as emotional support animals and service animals for people with disorders like PTSD—they're great at it. You might not be able to get a pet of your own, especially if you're still in college or you live somewhere that isn't pet-friendly, but there are still ways you can take advantage of this. Volunteering at a pet shelter, choosing to moonlight as a pet sitter on the weekends, or spending time with friends or family members with dogs can all help you reap the benefits of a quick puppy snuggle and assuage your frayed nerves.

Get Outside

Being outside is so good for us. Remember, we evolved to be outside, working, hunting, and farming. Nowadays, we spend so much of our time indoors, at school, or sitting at a desk at work, and it can really be draining. Getting outside can improve energy levels and help with burnout while also improving sleep quality. Your circadian rhythm, which regulates your sleep and wake cycles, relies on natural sunlight to manage your hormone levels, so getting out there is a great way to reset them. Go hiking, plant a garden, or just take a nice walk and bust that stress.

Breathing and Grounding

Having tools and tricks that can ground you help when your emotions run haywire. There are always times when we feel overwhelmed. Even the most organized of us, the ones who seem the most put together, have times when something seems impossible, or they're blinded with anger or burnt out so much that they just want to give up.

Various grounding techniques exist, from mindful meditation to yoga. One of my favorites is a trick that's easy to implement anywhere you go. It's called square breathing and you can do it in a meeting, driving your car, or just about anywhere else. All you have to do is a few quick deep breathing exercises and feel the benefits. It's discreet and suitable for those moments when you're out and about and just need to reset your mind.

To begin, you breathe deeply through your nose for four seconds. You hold your breath for four seconds, then exhale through your mouth for four seconds. Finally, hold it for four more seconds before starting over. It's called square breathing because it's paced out with four seconds per step. As you do this, you activate your parasympathetic nervous system, which is the part that controls your fight-or-flight response. By breathing calmly, you send messages to that part of your nervous system that says there's no danger here and it calms you down.

Chapter Summary

Being in control of yourself and your mind can be difficult at times, and without self-care, you can find yourself quickly burning out. Implementing a solid self-care routine is one of the best ways you can keep yourself grounded and feeling good about yourself. Grounding techniques, in particular, like deep breathing exercises, can help you when emotions run high and you find yourself feeling out of control. These can be particularly useful when you find yourself in stressful situations, like when you go to a doctor's office.

The next chapter focuses on handling medical matters of all kinds, including what to expect with health insurance, how to set up doctors' appointments, and when you need to be seen.

CHAPTER 12
MEDICAL MATTERS

One of the biggest changes that happen when you reach adulthood is that suddenly, you're responsible for your own health. You have to consent to treatments, you have medical privacy from your parents, and you get to make all the decisions. Depending on your agreement with your parents, you may also be responsible for paying for your care. This can feel like a pretty big responsibility, especially if your parents handled everything before.

When I turned 18, the revelation that I had to schedule my own appointments *terrified* me. Looking back on it, I'm not sure why it was such a problem for me, but I think a part of it was that I was intimidated by having to make the phone call, get myself to the appointment, and then be on my own for the appointment. While it had been years since my parents went into the room with me for most of my annual checkups, they still were present and could handle if any treatment was needed. It was far easier to pretend that I was healthy and therefore didn't need the appointments.

There's a problem with this line of thinking, though—when you don't get regular screenings and checkups, you can miss something important that would have otherwise been detected earlier. There are all sorts of symptoms that you might not be conscious of that can be detected in a blood test or physical exam. Missing preventative care can mean dealing with costlier care in the future.

Health Insurance

In the US, young adults can remain on their parent's health care plans until they turn 26, meaning that even if you're an adult and responsible for yourself financially, your parents can still keep you on their own insurance plans through work or that they pay for themselves. This is good news, too, because health insurance can be expensive. Even being on their plans, you still have to deal with deductibles, copays, and other costs associated with them.

In other areas of the world, health insurance may look different. Many countries have a nationalized health system where the cost of care is covered by the country. In Canada and several European countries, for example, public health care is free to everyone. The same goes for Australia and Brazil.

Important Terms in Health Insurance

Whether you have your own health insurance plan or rely on your parents', there are some terms you'll want to know in advance:

- ✧ **Deductible:** A deductible is an amount you have to cover for your health care before your insurance plan begins to pay. For example, if your plan has a $2,000 annual deductible, your health insurance won't start paying out on treatment until you've already spent and paid $2,000 out of pocket.

✧ **Copayment:** Even when insurance is covering the bill for your appointment, you may have a copayment (copay). This is the amount you pay as your portion of the bill. They can vary based on your plan.

✧ **Coinsurance:** Coinsurance refers to the share of the cost for covered services that you are responsible for. It's usually a set percentage in your plan.

✧ **Premium:** Each month, you or the policyholder have a premium. This is the amount you pay to keep your plan active.

✧ **Network:** Not all medical facilities accept all insurance, especially if you're in the United States. When a facility or doctor is in network, they accept your insurance.

✧ **Out-of-pocket maximum:** This is the most you'll pay out of pocket for your care for a calendar year. Once you reach the out-of-pocket maximum, your health insurance will cover the rest of the bills until the end of the year. You'll still owe your regular premium, but anything else should be covered if it's in network.

What if I Don't Have Health Insurance?

If, for whatever reason, you don't have health insurance, you can still go to the doctor if you need to be seen. However, you'll have to pay the office yourself for the services. This can be especially stressful for young adults who usually don't have a lot of money and can be a big reason for not going in for routine care. If you don't have insurance, you can be seen in the emergency room. You can't be turned away due to a lack of money if you truly need care.

Another consideration, if you don't currently have insurance, is looking into your state's Medicaid program or seeing what the cost for sliding scale insurance looks like. You might be able to get assistance with health care coverage this way.

Making a Doctor's Appointment

If you move for college, you may need to set up new health care local to you. Many college campuses have on-site health care available, or you can set up appointments around the area. When it's time to make a new appointment, find a doctor that accepts your insurance and meets your personal preferences. For example, if you're a woman and would prefer a woman treating you, or vice versa, for men, you can do that.

Then, you just follow some simple steps:

1. Call the office and inform them if you're a new patient. You may have to wait a week or two for a new patient appointment. If you're requesting care with a specific doctor, this is the time to bring it up.

2. Let the receptionist know why you need the appointment. It could be a checkup due to specific concerns like an illness or to have tests run.

3. Provide your insurance information.

4. Ask if you need to bring anything to the appointment, like records or a list of your prescriptions.

Sometimes, you'll have an appointment scheduled within a day or two, or it could be weeks or months, depending on the reason for the appointment and the doctor's availability. However, not all conditions can wait.

What to Do if the Problem Can't Wait for an Appointment

If you have to wait for a new patient appointment but have a pressing medical concern, you've got other options. Urgent care offices often allow you to be seen on the same day, which can be a great help if you think you have a minor infection or need antibiotics. Some common reasons people go to urgent care include:

- ✧ urinary tract infections
- ✧ a persistent cold or flu
- ✧ a minor injury like a sprain or strain
- ✧ stomach bugs or food poisoning
- ✧ sudden rashes or insect bites
- ✧ burns, cuts, or scrapes that need treatment but don't warrant going to the emergency room

Sometimes, going to the emergency room is the right answer for more serious conditions or injuries:

- ✧ sudden severe pain
- ✧ uncontrollable bleeding
- ✧ vision changes
- ✧ pain or pressure in the chest or upper abdomen
- ✧ altered consciousness, confusion, or disorientation, especially after a head injury

- ✧ vomiting or coughing up blood
- ✧ bright red blood in bowel movements
- ✧ shortness of breath or difficulty breathing
- ✧ severe headaches, especially with slurred speech or difficulty speaking
- ✧ dizziness, fainting, or weakness in half the body
- ✧ having a seizure for the first time, or for people who are known to have seizures, one that lasts longer than five minutes
- ✧ feeling like you want to hurt yourself or others
- ✧ severe injuries, including broken bones, head injuries, deep cuts, and severe burns
- ✧ severe, persistent vomiting or diarrhea

If you're not sure if something is ER-worthy, the best thing to do is call the hospital. They often have triage nurses available to speak to about whether you need to be seen immediately or if you can wait for an appointment.

Attending a Doctor's Appointment Alone

When appointment day rolls around, you might be nervous if you've never been responsible for getting yourself there alone before. With a bit of preparation and planning out what to expect and what to do, it's not so bad! It gets easier after the first few times, especially if you're prepared.

Be Early and Prepared

Make sure that you arrive at the office 10–15 minutes before your scheduled appointment time. You may need to fill out intake paperwork or you might get lost trying to get there. This 15-minute buffer helps in case of traffic or you get lost. Bring your ID, insurance card, and anything else the receptionist said that you needed when you scheduled your appointment, too.

Have Questions Ready

If you have any particular concerns before your appointment, write them down, along with any questions you may have. The appointment probably won't be very long, so you'll want to be able to efficiently go down the list and address all concerns.

Be Specific

When you describe symptoms and concerns to your doctor or nurse, be as specific as possible. It's best if you're able to tell them when the symptoms started, where the pain is, and anything you've done to try to alleviate them.

Chapter Summary

When you become an adult, you also inherit the responsibility for your health and well-being, something that, before this point, your parents were responsible for. As scary as it can be the first few times, it gets easier with practice! This is true of many things in life as you learn to readjust your expectations and keep pushing yourself out of your comfort zone.

The next section of this book focuses on personal development, including being able to learn and grow as a person. Personal development is all about learning, resilience, and recognizing that it's okay to be uncomfortable sometimes.

PART 5

PERSONAL DEVELOPMENT

Everyone thinks you make mistakes when you're young. But I don't think we make any fewer when we're grown up.

–Jodi Picoult

CHAPTER 13

TIME MANAGEMENT AND GOAL SETTING

We never get our time back. Once it's gone, it's gone for good. If you waste that time endlessly scrolling through TikTok or Facebook, that's time squandered that you may one day wish you had spent differently. Did you know that the average person uses social media for 2 hours and 31 minutes per day? How much is that in a year? Well, it's nearly 919 hours annually or the equivalent of 38.3 days around the clock. If we count just waking hours, averaging 16 per day, that number nearly doubles to 57 days. That's right, nearly two months of time each year is spent on social media on average.

What would you do with all that time if you had it? That's enough time to spend on hobbies, studies, or passions, and instead, it's wasted scrolling through things that you probably won't remember a few days later.

Social media, silly videos on the internet, and other time wasters sap away at what time we have, wasting it away. Wouldn't you rather do something productive with it instead?

Learning to balance your time is one of the most important parts of being an adult. As kids, we had our parents there to tell us what to do and when to do it. They could limit screen time and wasted hours by setting rules, but as soon as you enter adulthood, your time is your own and no one else's. What will you do with it?

Time is Money—Don't Waste It!

We've all heard people say that time is money, but it's actually quite true. Every hour you have is one that you can use to potentially earn or save money. A freed-up hour can be used to cook yourself a nutritious meal, saving money on eating out. An hour could be spent doing chores instead of outsourcing or working on your passion projects that could one day become your livelihood.

The worst thing you can do to yourself is waste your time. Sure, you can have fun and do things that you enjoy, but when you're constantly letting the little things eat away at your time, you're quite literally wasting your life away. The good news is that you can reclaim your time. You can put down the phone and stop doom-scrolling and instead direct your efforts to things that will be more productive.

Time Sinks to Avoid

Ready to figure out how much time you waste? We're going to go over a list of the most common time-wasters people in college tend to fall into. How many of them apply to you? How much time do you spend each day doing each of these activities? One or two little time wasters might not seem like a big deal, but if you're not careful, you can build habits that waste more time than you use to be productive. That's not to say that you have to be active and productive all the time—you need downtime to rest, too! But as they say, everything in moderation. Check out these common time wasters:

Binging TV Shows or Online Videos

Watching an episode of your favorite show is a great way to unwind after a long day. Watching hours of it while you try to do other things, on the other hand, can really just distract you. This is especially true if you're trying to study while watching a show. Stick to playing instrumental background music if you don't want to study in silence.

Studying Without a Plan

If you study without some sort of plan, you can find yourself wasting a lot of time. It's not enough to just read the textbook from start to finish, and when you have several classes to study for, you have to be intentional with your time.

Develop a study plan that outlines what you will do and when so you'll know how to tackle it all and best spend your time. For example:

- ✧ Take notes on the assigned chapter for psychology for 45 minutes.
- ✧ Study for the upcoming chemistry midterm for an hour.
- ✧ Spend half an hour working on a philosophy paper.

When you study with an intentional plan, it's much easier to make good progress.

Social Media

With so many social media platforms to browse, it can be easy to underestimate how much time you're actually spending on them. You might spend 20 minutes on Facebook, 30 minutes on Instagram, and another 30 minutes scrolling through TikTok and not realize just how much time you're spending. Then, add in notifications popping up and sucking you back in, or the time that you spend chatting with people on the platform and the amount of time balloons up pretty quickly.

Instead of using social media all day, disable the notifications and set specific times when you'll use the apps. You don't have to cut social media out cold turkey and it can be a great way to stay in touch with friends, but you shouldn't let it consume your life.

Procrastination

We all procrastinate from time to time, but if it's a habit for you to say that you'll do something later or tomorrow, you're probably wasting a lot of time while also putting some pretty stressful time crunches onto yourself as well. If you say you'll study later, you lose out on study time that you might have now and you may find yourself staying up later to get to it all. Or, if you say you'll do the dishes after work instead of before like you normally do, you may find yourself in a position where you don't have anything clean to make dinner with. Beating procrastination can be tough, but learning to do so is one of the most valuable tools you can teach yourself. If you have to do something that will take less than five minutes, do it immediately instead of putting it off.

Schedules, tools like the Pomodoro method (more on this later!), and breaking down tasks into smaller steps so they don't feel so overwhelming can all help you beat procrastination.

Overplanning

Are you an overplanner? A lot of us are—we spend inordinate amounts of time trying to make sure that every last detail of our plans are going to go off without a hitch that we run out of time to actually properly execute it. Or, all that overplanning can lead us to give up when whatever it was doesn't go exactly according to plan.

Trying to Make Things Perfect

If that last point resonated with you, you might also spend a lot of time agonizing over the tiniest details of whatever you're doing. If it's not exactly right, you might focus endlessly on a small detail that really isn't very important.

There's no such thing as perfection, meaning it's useless to waste your time trying to achieve it. Instead, focus on setting realistic standards and let go of the small details. No one cares if the sandwich you make doesn't look perfect if it still tastes good.

Unclear Goals

Setting goals that aren't efficient is another way that a lot of people waste their time. We'll be talking about setting effective goals later in this chapter. When your goals are unnecessarily vague, like "I want to lose weight" or "I want to eat more vegetables," you don't really give yourself something concrete to work toward, and we'll talk about addressing that shortly.

Multitasking

We often think that multitasking is the perfect way to squeeze more into a short period of time, but the truth is this is incredibly inefficient. Your brain can only really focus on one thing at a time, which means when you're multitasking, you are constantly forcing your brain to shift gears, which can quickly draw things out and cost you time.

It's better to focus on one task at a time, giving it your full attention, rather than trying to do several things at once. If you're in a position where you feel like you have to multitask, try breaking down the task into something more manageable. The more you streamline your process, the quicker you'll get things done, and the more time you'll save!

How to Manage Your Time

As you start saving time, you'll better be able to manage it. For most young adults, college is the first real test they get at managing their time by themselves, and that freedom can be addictive. There's no one telling you what to do, when to study, or how to live. The problem is, if you've never had the experience of managing your time yourself or facing the consequences of poor time management, you're at risk of completely dropping the ball.

It took me a solid two weeks after I moved into my dorm to realize that my time management was *horrible*. I'd put off my studying or homework assignments until the last minute, which meant my first few grades in my classes were much lower than what I was used to. I'd prioritize having fun and making friends rather than getting to the tasks I needed to handle. By the end of my second week, I was exhausted and staring at a whole mess of studying, chores, and other responsibilities.

Part of the reason I struggled so much was that when I lived with my parents, they had me on a structured schedule. I had to complete my homework before I could go out with friends. I had to do my chores beforehand, too. All the structure they built into my life felt like a big drag when I was a teen, but once I got to college, I realized that they were really just trying to help me out and set me up for success.

While my first semester of college ended with grades lower than I was used to, it also gave me a solid understanding of what it's like to be an adult. I needed to manage my time because no one else would do it for me. I had to take responsibility for those lower grades, and by the time the second semester rolled around, I had the solid schedule and foundation I needed to succeed.

My recommendation for time management is to have a predictable schedule and stick to it. Anything that you need to do should be prioritized in the level of importance to you, which means that you'll have to make those major decisions for yourself.

For example, you might really want to go to that party, but you have to be up early the next morning for your weekend job. What's more important to you? You may decide that you still want to go to the party, but you also don't want to be exhausted, so you decide to go home early instead of partying into the wee hours of the morning.

Prioritize Your Work

Prioritizing your work is all about figuring out what needs to be done immediately and what can wait or be eliminated entirely. When it feels like you're drowning in work, make a list of all the tasks you're trying to squeeze in. Then, start rating them by their urgency.

Unimportant tasks, like endless time scrolling through social media, can be put off or don't matter to you.

Important tasks matter to you or need to be done. These could be your hobbies, studying, working, or completing your chores. They need to be scheduled somewhere during your day and completed in a timely manner.

Urgent tasks are things that have to be done to avoid issues. This could be completing an assignment for school, studying for an impending test, or getting car maintenance done to keep your car running. Many of these tasks could be things that were once important that you decided to push off until you couldn't any longer.

One of the best solutions to having a buildup of tasks is to avoid procrastinating. We'll have some tips for time management and beating procrastination shortly.

Don't Overcommit

Saying no when you're asked to do something can be difficult, especially if you fall into people-pleasing habits. The problem with this comes when you start getting overwhelmed with commitments. Life is busy enough on its own, with work, school, and maintaining a social life. There's no need to make it worse by taking on every little favor that people ask you to do.

Or, maybe you're already overcommitted because you thought you'd have the time to do everything, only to find out that it all piled up on you. I get it—as a busy parent, I'm constantly inundated with all the things needed from me for work, my children, and my husband. There's always laundry to do, homework to complete, extracurriculars to drive to, and more. In college, it seemed like there was just as much going on. I had to study, work, and still find time for my friends.

It's okay to say no to things that you don't have the time or bandwidth to complete. Let go of the things that don't matter to you or that you simply can't dedicate your time to. Yes, this might mean letting go of some things that are important, like foregoing a favorite club on campus to go to work sometimes or not going out with friends every night, but it'll help you to balance your schedule.

By avoiding the trap of overcommitting, you free up time that can better be utilized doing important and urgent things on your list. All you'll need to do is use that time wisely and efficiently.

Pomodoro Technique

One of my absolute favorite ways of being efficient with time is using the Pomodoro Technique to manage my time without feeling like I'm overwhelmed or like I don't have time to relax. As a fun aside, the technique got its name from the Italian word for tomato because the person who mainstreamed it used a kitchen timer shaped like a tomato to break up his time.

With this technique, you are breaking up your time into 25-minute stretches of working on something with a 5-minute break. After four intervals, you get a 15- or 30-minute break to unwind.

This helps by breaking down what otherwise feels like a long, unbearable task and turning it into smaller chunks that feel more manageable. That means less time dwelling on how long it will take, feeling overwhelmed and procrastinating, and more time doing what you need to do.

Get started by choosing a task you need to complete, like a paper, or choosing to study something or a chore. Set a timer for 25 minutes and work the whole time. Don't get distracted, leave your phone somewhere you won't be tempted by it, and get going. When the timer goes off, give yourself that quick break. I like to write down my progress as I go so I can see how productive I've been while I use this method. If I'm reading or writing, I jot down my word count or how many pages I got through and then unwind. After your short break is over, set up the timer and start again. I'd bet this will help save time by keeping you on task!

Time-Saving Tips

Still feel tight on time after implementing these changes? These are some of my favorite tips I used in college and still use today to make the most out of my time:

✧ **Pay attention to your time:** I like to keep track of my time by making sure I'm conscious of how long I spend on my biggest time wasters. For me, checking my phone is absolutely one of the worst. When I feel like my time is getting out of control, I take a look at my phone's apps to see just how long I spend on it. The number can be pretty scary sometimes and it reminds me to set it down and focus on what's going on around me instead.

✧ **Use downtime to your advantage:** Do you commute to work or school? Whether you walk, ride a bus, or drive, you can always boost your productivity with audiobooks. Or, if you take the bus or carpool, you can use the time you spend traveling to study, catch up on work, or tend to some of your planning for the week. Instead of just waiting around, get productive instead!

✧ **Separate work and pleasure:** We associate our spaces with what we do most in them, so separating where you work from where you sleep or enjoy yourself can help put you into the productive mindset by association. This could be tough if you have a dorm, but you could choose to do most of your studying in the library on campus. Dedicate a set office for yourself in your home if you've got the luxury to do so.

- ✧ **Outsource if you can:** This might be kind of hard, depending on where you are in your life. Some things can be outsourced, and if you have the ability to do so, you should. For students, a major source of outsourcing is eating in the school dining halls. You don't have to cook or clean up after yourself.

- ✧ **Find tools to help you:** Let me tell you—when I first heard about robot vacuums, I thought it was a ridiculous luxury and a waste of time and money. Now, with children and pets? I couldn't imagine it any other way. These tools are my livelihood and keep me grounded. If there are tools that will boost your productivity and they're affordable to you, they're probably worth the investment.

As you implement these tools, you can remain focused on what matters the most. Then, you just have to make sure you have the goals to roadmap your plan forward.

SMART Goals Keep You Focused

We already introduced the topic of SMART goals earlier when talking about self-care, but now it's time to go in-depth with them. As stated earlier, SMART goals are specific, measurable, achievable, relevant, and timely.

The reason I like these goals is that it keeps me focused. When writing goals in this format, it's much easier to see exactly what needs to be done by which date or time to stay on track. As a result, I'm able to focus so much more on what needs to be done without getting stuck with tasks that suddenly become urgent or necessary to complete quickly to meet requirements.

✧ **Specific:** Goals should be very specific. For example, if your goal is to get good grades in college, you don't really have a metric that tells you what you're aiming for. What's a good grade to you?

✧ **Measurable:** By making your goal measurable, you give yourself something that has a definitive ending. This could be getting a 3.5 GPA or not getting below an 80% on an assignment for the semester.

✧ **Achievable:** Goals need to be achievable, too. You can't, for example, say you want to graduate with a 4.0 GPA when you already have below that, or you want to run a marathon in a week when you're currently living a relatively inactive life. Make sure you're realistic about what you can and can't do when you set your goal. It should be something that's a bit of a stretch and makes you work for it, but not something you can never do. How will you achieve it? If you want to get that 3.5 GPA, what's your study plan? How many classes will you take at once?

✧ **Relevant:** Your goal also needs to be relevant to you. Is it something you'd willingly do? Do you have an interest in doing it? If you genuinely don't care about college, for example, because you plan on going into a career that doesn't require a degree, are you really going to give it your all?

✧ **Timely:** Finally, your goal needs to have some sort of finality to it. There has to be a deadline on it so you know whether you've succeeded or failed. This could be graduation if you want that high GPA or an arbitrary date you've set. This will help keep you accountable and working toward your goal.

When you set up your goal, start by writing down each step. What do you want? How will you achieve it? Why does it matter to you? When do you need to be done with your work toward it? These things matter, and writing them all down will help paint a clearer picture of what you'll need to do and how to schedule it all into your plan.

Chapter Summary

A major part of personal development is being able to stick to schedules and manage your time wisely. When you can mitigate time sinks and focus on SMART goals, you can push yourself forward, learning more and working toward being more successful. From there, it's all about resilience and remembering that it's okay to be a work in progress. It's okay to not be able to do everything right the first time, and developing a growth mindset, which we'll introduce in the next chapter, is all about getting back up when we fall.

CHAPTER 14

GROWTH MINDSET, SELF-CONFIDENCE, AND RESILIENCE

With tools for managing your time in place, you can start tackling your goals and bringing them to fruition. It's so fulfilling to see all your hard work bear fruitful results! As you achieve your goals, you'll likely find yourself feeling more confident and capable in your life. The key here, though, is recognizing that when you do fail at something (and it will happen, I promise!), you can keep moving forward.

One of the hardest things in life to learn is to be resilient. Resilience requires you to be confident and recognize that failing at something isn't the worst thing in the world. In fact, failure is what propels growth. If you didn't fail at something, how do you know that what you were doing wasn't too easy for you?

Something I had to learn with my kids is that praising them for every single thing they did right wasn't the right path to building confidence. In fact, the more I praised them for getting things done correctly, the more resistant they were to try new things. When I talked to them about it, what they said surprised me: They were afraid that if they messed up, I wouldn't give them the praise, and I'd be disappointed in them. In other words, they were afraid of failure and what I'd do if they struggled, so they resisted trying new things and challenging themselves. Instead of teaching them to be confident, bold children who wanted to tackle everything life had to offer, they wanted to stay firmly in their comfort zone.

Your Brain Never Stops Growing

If staying in your comfort zone resonates with you, you're not alone. Looking back on it, I was the same way when I was younger. I was afraid of making mistakes because mistakes meant I was wrong, and being wrong meant I wasn't right and I hated not being right. It was a dangerous thought spiral. I thought that if I just didn't try, I couldn't fail, but this is the wrong way to look at it. You don't fail at something until you give up on it. By never being willing to try something, I was inadvertently failing by default, but somehow convinced myself it wasn't the same thing.

Developing a Growth Mindset

Part of what builds resilience is to develop a growth mindset. Resilience is the ability to bounce back from failure and keep moving toward your goal. It's okay to be disappointed that you didn't succeed, but what's more important is recognizing that you can keep working in the future to see better results.

In other words, just because you didn't succeed today doesn't mean that you won't succeed in the future. This is because your brain never stops growing. It's like a muscle in the sense that the more that you work it, the stronger it becomes. It's never too late to learn a new skill or achieve new goals, and it's only natural not to be very good at something when you first start.

Imagine if we all gave up the first time we tried and failed something. Babies would never crawl or walk. We'd never talk or read or write because all of these are learned skills that have a lot of failure at the beginning. Doctors would never perform surgery or help heal people. Lawyers would give up in law school the first time they misremembered something.

We all fail from time to time. We all get things wrong every now and then. And that's okay.

When we focus on a growth mindset, we don't look at the results as much as we look at the effort put into it. After all, it's the effort that really deserves the praise—it's all the hard work you put into getting to that end goal that really matters. Yes, it's great that you succeeded, but that success is meaningful and satisfying because you worked for it.

If you shift your mindset to focus on the effort you put into a situation instead of the end result, you find that it's easier to bounce back after getting an undesired result. Instead of thinking that where you're at in that moment in terms of skill level is it, you'll see that you can keep learning and growing. In other words, you become resilient, and that resilience will help keep you moving forward with your life.

Tips to Develop a Growth Mindset for Resilience

If you're the kind of person to crumble at the thought of failure, don't worry—you can change your mindset. After all, that's what this is all about, right? Developing a growth mindset both requires and develops resilience. The more you practice, the easier it will become, just like with any other type of exercise. Only this time, you're exercising your brain.

Embrace Your Imperfections

You don't have to be perfect. In fact, your imperfections are valuable parts of who you are and how much room you still have to grow. When you get something wrong, it's not a ding against who you are as a person. It's not a sign that you're useless or stupid. It's just a sign that you don't know that information or skill *yet*. You see, the "yet" is important here.

Just because you don't know something today doesn't mean you won't know it in the future. Remind yourself of this when you make mistakes. Instead of beating yourself up, say, "I don't know this yet, but I can learn."

See Challenges as Opportunities

When something is difficult, it's not a sign of you being inadequate, either. It's actually a really good opportunity for you to begin learning and for you to grow. Every challenge, every mishap along the way, is a way you can move forward and develop as a person. I'll bet you didn't know algebra when you stepped into class for the first time, but by the time you left, your skills had grown dramatically. Everything is like that. It's not raw talent that makes us successful—it's how we handle the challenges and use them to grow along the way.

Focus on Positive Language

So much of what makes up our mindsets is how we speak, both about ourselves and about the world around us. When you use negative language, like "I'm never going to figure this out," you're putting yourself in a precarious position. How much effort do you think you'll really put into figuring out whatever it is if you don't think you can actually do it? You might make a halfhearted attempt, but to really put your all into something, you have to believe that you can do it.

Get rid of absolutes in your language. There's no "always" or "never" or black and white. The world is more than shades of gray, too. We live in a vibrant world filled with spectrums of color, just like we ourselves have spectrums of abilities. You add or take away a little light to a color and what you're left with changes. Likewise, your abilities are the same way. They aren't stagnant and they can change based on what you put into them.

The more you make yourself comfortable with positive language, the better you will feel. Even better, the more confident you can grow. Growth mindsets and positive mindsets leave us feeling better about ourselves, granting us the key to success.

Self-Confidence and Success

Self-confidence is what gives you faith that you can succeed. It's what allows you to keep on trudging through the hard times and to trust yourself enough to know that you'll make the choices that are right for you. It also assures you that even if you don't have the answers now, you'll be able to come up with the answers with a little bit of effort.

In other words, self-confidence is having trust in yourself. It's not the same thing as being overconfident, where you overestimate your abilities. Rather, when you're self-confident, you're well aware of what you can do. This comes with all sorts of benefits that will help you through your life and take you on the pathway to success.

Self-confidence shows in how we present ourselves to others, how we hold our bodies, and how we approach problems. That inner confidence tells people they can put their confidence in you too. The result? People with self-confidence are more likely to get raises and promotions when they interview. They're also, as a result, more likely to be successful.

The good news here is that self-confidence is something we learn. Some people might be naturally more self-confident than others, but that doesn't mean that you can't grow it too. Growth mindset, remember?

Trial and Error and Trial Some More

Self-confidence is all about being able to pick yourself back up again when you fall. It's being able to trust your abilities. That doesn't mean that you trust that you're perfect already—it's about being aware of what they truly are and what you can do to continue learning and growing.

If you're not confident yet, all you need to do is to keep on trying, even in the face of challenges. This is a cycle of trial and error. Each error brings you another step closer to finding your solution. It's like being a scientist—you know what you want to do, and then you have to experiment to find the answer. Every time you try something that doesn't work, you know that it's time to try something different. Eventually, you'll get it right.

The more you work at this, remembering that you have a growth mindset and that you can continue to learn as long as you live and keep trying, the more confident you'll become. You'll become comfortable with making mistakes or failing, recognizing the silver lining of learning that comes with it. As you become more comfortable, you'll also be able to explore more, opening up doors that you never knew existed in your future.

Step Out of Your Comfort Zone

Self-confidence helps us step out of our comfort zone because we know we can trust ourselves to navigate through it, no matter what happens. It's the ability to trust that there are more things to learn and that sometimes, the learning and growing process is uncomfortable. However, resilience helps us through.

I've had to step out of my comfort zone countless times throughout life, applying for jobs, deciding to have children, making moves across the country... It can be intimidating or even terrifying when you face the unknown. But, it's only unknown for as long as you let it be.

The funny thing about stepping out of your comfort zone is that the more you do it, the easier it becomes and the more confident you feel. That's why I like to try new things all the time. I might try cooking a new meal with a technique I've never tried before or going to a new activity. There's something awe-inspiring about facing something brand new and slowly but surely learning how to actually do it. It's like being a child again, growing and learning.

Just because your body finishes growing doesn't mean your mind has to, and the more you try new things and stick to them, even when they're hard, the more likely you are to succeed. After all, you miss 100% of the shots you don't take. Your chances are infinitely higher just by trying, even if they're still low. And the more you practice, the easier those shots will get over time.

Chapter Summary

Developing a growth mindset and having the self-confidence and resilience to continue in the face of failure are the keys to success. When you learn to pick yourself up after you fall, you grow as a person, and that growth is priceless. You'll be able to step out of your comfort zone and thrive. Remember that failure isn't concrete until you give up. Until then, any mistakes and mishaps along the way are just speed bumps on your path to success.

CONCLUSION

> *Relax. You will become an adult. You will figure out your career. You will find someone who loves you. You have a whole lifetime; time takes time. The only way to fail at life is to abstain.*

–Johanna de Silentio

The thing no one ever tells you about growing up is that it's not about knowing everything there is to know or being right all the time. There's never going to be a time when you feel perfectly equipped to take on everything the world has to throw your way. No—growing up is learning how to navigate through it all, even when you don't have the solutions. It's about learning to stand on your own two feet as an independent adult, but that doesn't mean that you have to face the world alone.

Rely on your loved ones. Build a social safety net of people you trust. Keep on learning, even when things are tough at first. Foster that growth mindset until the idea of failing isn't scary anymore. Put all these skills to the test and keep on practicing them.

You'll make mistakes. You'll probably miss a bill or two by accident (but I really hope you don't!). Things won't always work out as planned, but that's life. As you work on yourself and your skills, you'll keep learning. You'll grow. You'll *thrive.* All you have to do is remember not to give up.

Adulthood can be scary. After all, there's a lot riding on you that you'll have to figure out. However, I know that you can do it. We all can. Keep up the good work. Don't be afraid to ask questions or for help. And most importantly, have the confidence in yourself that you can, and will, succeed in this life, no matter where it takes you. Whether you enter the workforce immediately, decide to run your own business, go to college, or pursue a trade, you can do it. You just have to remember to pick yourself back up again when you fall. If you can do that, you're already halfway there. Good luck and happy adulting!

THANK YOU

Thank you so much for purchasing my book.

The marketplace is filled with dozens and dozens of other similar books but you took a chance and chose this one. And I hope it was well worth it.

So again, THANK YOU for getting this book and for making it all the way to the end.

Before you go, I wanted to ask you for one small favor.

Could you please consider posting a review for my book on the platform? Posting a review is the best and easiest way to support the work of independent authors like me.

Your feedback will help me to keep writing the kind of books that will help you get the results you want. It would mean a lot to me to hear from you.

Leave a Review on Amazon US →

Leave a Review on Amazon UK→

ABOUT THE AUTHOR

Emily Carter is an author who loves helping teens with their biggest turn point in life, adulting. She grew up in New York and is happily married to her high school sweetheart. She also has two own children.

In her free time, Emily is an avid volunteer at a local food bank and enjoys hiking, traveling, and reading books on personal development. With over a decade of experience in the education and parenting field she has seen the difference that good parenting and the right tips can make in a teenager's life. She is now an aspiring writer through which she shares her insights and advice on raising happy, healthy, and resilient children, teens and young adults.

Emily's own struggles with navigating adulthood and overcoming obstacles inspired her to write. She noticed a gap in education regarding teaching essential life skills to teens and young adults, and decided to write comprehensive guides covering everything from money and time management to job searching and communication skills. Emily hopes her book will empower teens and young adults to live their best lives and reach their full potential.

REFERENCES

Adulthood quotes (546 Quotes). (n.d.). Www.goodreads.com. Retrieved May 18, 2023, from https://www.goodreads. com/quotes/tag/adulthood?page=2

AdventHealth. (2019, March 19). *Don't wait: 15 reasons to head to the emergency room*. AdventHealth. https://www. adventhealth.com/hospital/adventhealth-new-smyrna- beach/blog/dont-wait-15-reasons-head-emergency- room

Allen, S. (2022, June 2). *10 ways to save time every day that most people ignore*. Grammarly. https://www.grammarly. com/blog/save-time/

ASI Hastings. (2021, August 1). *The most effective way to clean a p-trap*. ASI Hastings. https://www.asiheatingandair. com/info/the-most-effective-way-to-clean-a-p-trap/

Ates, K. (2021, April 7). *Normal wear and tear vs. property damage: a landlord's guide*. Rentspree. https://www. rentspree.com/blog/normal-wear-and-tear

Bank of America. (2022). *Saving money tips - 8 simple ways to save money*. Better Money Habits. https://

bettermoneyhabits.bankofamerica.com/en/saving-budgeting/ways-to-save-money

Banton, C. (2023, March 28). *Interest rate*. Investopedia. https://www.investopedia.com/terms/i/interestrate.asp

Better Health. (2014). *Relationships and communication*. Better Health Channel. https://www.betterhealth.vic.gov.au/health/healthyliving/relationships-and-communication

Boogaard, K. (2021, December 26). *Write achievable goals with the SMART goals framework*. Atlassian. https://www.atlassian.com/blog/productivity/how-to-write-smart-goals

Boundaries: What are they and how to create them. (2022, February 25). University of Illinois Chicago Wellness Center. https://wellnesscenter.uic.edu/news-stories/boundaries-what-are-they-and-how-to-create-them/

Brown, T., & Finch, S. (2022, September 27). *How to rent your first apartment: apartment guide and checklist*. Apartment List. https://www.apartmentlist.com/renter-life/first-time-renter-apartment-guide-checklist

Businessman with an affliction quotes by Anas Hamshari. (n.d.). Www.goodreads.com. https://www.goodreads.com/work/quotes/85599385-businessman-with-an-affliction

CDC. (2017). *CDC - How much sleep do I need? - sleep and sleep disorders*. CDC. https://www.cdc.gov/sleep/about_sleep/how_much_sleep.html

CDC. (2021a, March 1). *Healthy eating tips*. CDC. https://www.cdc.gov/nccdphp/dnpao/features/healthy-eating-tips/index.html

CDC. (2021b, May 16). *Benefits of healthy eating*. CDC; U.S. Department of Health & Human Services. https://www.cdc.gov/nutrition/resources-publications/benefits-of-healthy-eating.html

CDC. (2022a, June 2). *How much physical activity do adults need?* CDC. https://www.cdc.gov/physicalactivity/basics/adults/index.htm

CDC. (2022b, September 13). *Sleep hygiene tips - sleep and sleep disorders*. CDC. https://www.cdc.gov/sleep/about_sleep/sleep_hygiene.html

Chen, J. (2020, April 9). *Lease definition and complete guide to renting*. Investopedia. https://www.investopedia.com/terms/l/lease.asp

Clear, J. (2014, January 23). *The marshmallow experiment and the power of delayed gratification*. James Clear. https://jamesclear.com/delayed-gratification

Collins, C. (2020, April 21). *The importance of self confidence for your success*. Mom's Got Money. https://www.momsgotmoney.com/the-importance-of-self-confidence/

Compound interest calculator. (n.d.). Www.investor.gov. https://www.investor.gov/financial-tools-calculators/calculators/compound-interest-calculator

Cuncic, A. (2022, November 9). *How to practice active listening.* Verywell Mind. https://www.verywellmind.com/what-is-active-listening-3024343

Davenport, B. (2020, May 31). *21 examples of healthy boundaries in relationships.* Live Bold and Bloom. https://liveboldandbloom.com/05/relationships/healthy-boundaries-in-relationships

Davis, T. (2018, December 28). *Self-care: 12 ways to take better care of yourself.* Psychology Today. https://www.psychologytoday.com/us/blog/click-here-happiness/201812/self-care-12-ways-take-better-care-yourself

DeNicola, L. (2023, January 11). *Miss a credit card payment? Here's what you can do.* Intuit Credit Karma. https://www.creditkarma.com/credit-cards/i/what-happens-if-you-miss-a-credit-card-payment

Dieker, N. (2022, January 18). *What credit score do you start with?* Bankrate. https://www.bankrate.com/personal-finance/credit/what-credit-score-do-you-start-with/

Do other countries have credit scores? (n.d.). Chase. https://www.chase.com/personal/credit-cards/education/credit-score/do-other-countries-have-credit-scores

Dweck, C. (2016, January 13). *What having a "growth mindset" actually means.* Harvard Business Review. https://hbr.org/2016/01/what-having-a-growth-mindset-actually-means

Feuerman, M. (2017, November 9). *Managing vs. resolving conflict in relationships: The blueprints for success.* The Gottman Institute. https://www.gottman.com/blog/managing-vs-resolving-conflict-relationships-blueprints-success/

Field, B. (2022, November 16). *7 surprising ways to make your relationship even better.* Verywell Mind. https://www.verywellmind.com/7-surprising-ways-to-make-your-relationship-better-5094212

Folger, J. (2022, December 10). *Tips for successful retirement investing.* Investopedia. https://www.investopedia.com/articles/personal-finance/111313/six-critical-rules-successful-retirement-investing.asp

Fontinelle, A. (2018). *8 financial tips for young adults.* Investopedia. https://www.investopedia.com/articles/younginvestors/08/eight-tips.asp

Fontinelle, A. (2021, May 17). *10 reasons to use your credit card.* Investopedia. https://www.investopedia.com/articles/pf/10/credit-card-debit-card.asp

Food for teenagers: meal plan on the cheap! (2021, January 18). Shelf Cooking. https://shelfcooking.com/food-for-teenagers/

Freer, J. (2022, July 1). *Apartment maintenance - what is it and who is responsible for it?* ApartmentAdvisor. https://www.apartmentadvisor.com/blog/post/apartment-maintenance-what-is-it-and-who-is-responsible-for-it

Georgiev, D. (2023, February 28). *How much time do people spend on social media in 2023?* Tech Jury. https://techjury. net/blog/time-spent-on-social-media/#gref

Glowiak, M. (2020, April 14). *What is self-care and why is it important for you?* SNHU. https://www.snhu.edu/about-us/newsroom/health/what-is-self-care

Gomstyn, A. (2019). *Food for your mood: how what you eat affects your mental health.* Aetna. https://www.aetna. com/health-guide/food-affects-mental-health.html

Gould, W. R. (2021, November 9). *10 red flags in relationships.* Verywell Mind. https://www.verywellmind.com/10-red-flags-in-relationships-5194592

Gupta, S. (2021, December 27). *How to build trust in a relationship.* Verywell Mind. https://www.verywellmind.com/how-to-build-trust-in-a-relationship-5207611

Harvard School of Public Health. (2019, June 3). *Potassium.* The Nutrition Source. https://www.hsph.harvard.edu/ nutritionsource/potassium/

Health care for young adults findings and recommendations from the report investing in the health and well-being of young adults. (n.d.). https://nap.nationalacademies.org/ resource/18869/YAs_Health_Care_brief.pdf

Healthwise Staff. (2022, February 9). *Time management for teens: care instructions.* Myhealth.alberta.ca. https:// myhealth.alberta.ca/Health/aftercareinformation/pages/ conditions.aspx?hwid=ug6046

Healthy boundaries for teens. (n.d.). Crime Victim Center of Erie County. Retrieved May 13, 2023, from https://cvcerie. org/healthy-boundaries-for-teens/

Hill, L. (2021, April 22). *Breakfast: is it the most important meal?* WebMD. https://www.webmd.com/food-recipes/ breakfast-lose-weight

Holly. (2020, July 23). *Creating a house cleaning schedule that works.* Simplify Create Inspire. https://www. simplifycreateinspire.com/daily-weekly-monthly-cleaning-schedule/

How are FICO scores calculated?. (2018, October 19). MyFICO. https://www.myfico.com/credit-education/whats-in-your-credit-score#:~:text=FICO%20Scores%20are%20 calculated%20using

How health insurance works. (2020, April 13). Blue Cross NC. https://www.bluecrossnc.com/understanding-health-insurance/how-health-insurance-works

How to change a home air filter. (n.d.). The Home Depot. https:// www.homedepot.com/c/ah/how-to-change-a-home-air-filter/9ba683603be9fa5395fab906a15a05f

How to clean the inside of your washer and dryer. (n.d.). Www. appliancewhse.com. https://www.appliancewhse.com/ Content.aspx?ID=25

How to improve communication skills in your relationship. (n.d.). The Jed Foundation. https://jedfoundation.org/ resource/how-to-improve-communication-skills-in-your-relationship/

How to make a meal plan. (n.d.). Safefood. https://www.safefood.net/how-to/meal-plan

How to understand your costs and key health insurance terms. (2018, March 8). HealthCare.gov. https://www.healthcare.gov/blog/understand-health-insurance-definitions/

How to use a plumbing snake and when it's necessary. (2021, September 28). WM Buffington Company. https://wmbuffingtoncompany.com/blog/plumbing/when-and-how-to-use-drain-snake/

In and Out Express Care. (2019, March 3). *Top 9 reasons to go to urgent care - common urgent care complaints.* In and out Express Care. https://inandoutexpresscare.com/top-9-reasons-for-an-urgent-care-visit/

Keech, D. (2022, October 31). *15 home maintenance tasks and repairs everyone should know how to do.* Military by Owner. https://blog.militarybyowner.com/15-home-maintenance-tasks-and-repairs-everyone-should-know-how-to-do

Kellogg, K. (2021, February 10). *How to clean a dishwasher (quickly!).* Architectural Digest. https://www.architecturaldigest.com/story/how-to-clean-a-dishwasher-with-vinegar

Kilkus, J. (2022, March 27). *Is the mind-body connection real?* Psychology Today. https://www.psychologytoday.com/us/blog/navigating-cancer/202203/is-the-mind-body-connection-real

Lake, R. (2023, April 28). *How do credit cards work?* Investopedia. https://www.investopedia.com/how-do-credit-cards-work-5025119

Lawler, M. (2022, August 26). *How to start a self-care routine you'll follow.* EverydayHealth. https://www.everydayhealth.com/self-care/start-a-self-care-routine/

Lawler, M. (2023, March 17). *What is self-care, and why is it so important for your health?* Everyday Health. https://www.everydayhealth.com/self-care/

Lyons, M. (2021, December 9). *How to ground yourself: 14 techniques you need to try.* Www.betterup.com. https://www.betterup.com/blog/how-to-ground-yourself

Making an appointment. (2014, August 21). HealthCare. gov. https://www.healthcare.gov/blog/making-an-appointment/

Manolas, K. (2022, October 25). *Rental scams: how to spot them & what to do.* Avail. https://www.avail.co/education/guides/a-tenants-guide-to-finding-an-apartment/how-to-spot-a-rental-scam

McQuitty Hindmarsh, L. (2023, March 1). *20+ freezer essentials for a well stocked freezer.* Mums Make Lists. https://www.mumsmakelists.com/freezer-essentials/

Medcalf, A. (2022, August 2). *How to be honest and build trust in a relationship.* Abby Medcalf. https://abbymedcalf.com/how-to-be-honest-and-build-trust-in-a-relationship-2/

National Institute of Mental Health. (2021). *Caring for your mental health*. National Institute of Mental Health. https://www.nimh.nih.gov/health/topics/caring-for-your-mental-health

O'Shea, B. (2022, August 30). *What is a good credit score?* NerdWallet. https://www.nerdwallet.com/article/finance/what-is-a-good-credit-score

Pant, P. (n.d.). *How much should I save? 50 30 20 Rule*. TIAA. https://www.tiaa.org/public/learn/personal-finance-101/how-much-of-my-income-should-i-save-every-month

Parker-Pope, T. (2019). *How to have a better relationship*. The New York Times. https://www.nytimes.com/guides/well/how-to-have-a-better-relationship

Parrish, M. (2022, May 13). *How to help students develop a growth mindset*. Good Grief. https://good-grief.org/ways-to-develop-a-growth-mindset/

Peddicord, K. (2020, October 2). *12 rules for renting a home oversees*. U.S. News & World Report. https://money.usnews.com/money/retirement/baby-boomers/articles/rules-for-renting-a-home-overseas

Petersen, L. (2019, January 24). *Strengths of compromise as a conflict resolution*. Chron. https://smallbusiness.chron.com/strengths-compromise-conflict-resolution-10502.html

A quote by Eleanor Brown. (n.d.). Www.goodreads.com. Retrieved May 13, 2023, from https://www.goodreads.

com/quotes/9752464-self-care-is-not-selfish-you-cannot-serve-from-an-empty

A quote from Nineteen Minutes. (n.d.). Www.goodreads.com. Retrieved May 13, 2023, from https://www.goodreads.com/quotes/75688-everyone-thinks-you-make-mistakes-when-you-re-young-but-i

Ramsey Solutions. (2023, March 15). *How to save money: 22 simple tips.* Ramsey Solutions. https://www.ramseysolutions.com/budgeting/the-secret-to-saving-money

Robinson, L., Segal, J., & Smith, M. (2019). *Effective communication.* Help Guide. https://www.helpguide.org/articles/relationships-communication/effective-communication.htm

Rose, G. (2023, April 6). *Buying life insurance as an investment.* NerdWallet. https://www.nerdwallet.com/article/insurance/life-insurance-as-an-investment

Rosen, T. (2021, January 22). *Tips for going to the doctor by yourself as a college student.* Bwog - Columbia Student News. https://bwog.com/2021/01/tips-for-going-to-the-doctor-by-yourself-as-a-college-student/

Rudd, L. (2017, April 12). *How to change a light bulb. Living - Your Home, DIY and Life.* HomeServe. https://www.homeserve.com/uk/living/how-to/how-to-change-a-light-bulb/

Ryan, A. (2020, May 28). *Tips for your young adult and their 1st apartment.* Simply Family Magazine. https://

simplyfamilymagazine.com/tips-for-your-young-adult-and-their-1st-apartment

Saraev, N. (2022, May 19). *The top 10 most common time wasters & how to avoid them*. Day.io. https://day.io/blog/the-top-10-most-common-time-wasters-how-to-avoid-them/

Saving and investing for your future. (2022). University of Minnesota Extension. https://extension.umn.edu/personal-finances/saving-and-investing-your-future

Security deposit laws by state. (n.d.). Rocket Lawyer. Retrieved May 13, 2023, from https://www.rocketlawyer.com/real-estate/landlords/property-management/legal-guide/security-deposit-laws-by-state

Segal, J., Robinson, L., & Smith, M. (2019, March 21). *Conflict resolution skills*. HelpGuide. https://www.helpguide.org/articles/relationships-communication/conflict-resolution-skills.htm

17 relationship communication quotes every couple will love. (2021, February 16). The Healthy. https://www.thehealthy.com/family/relationships/relationship-communication-quotes/

Sharp Emerson, M. (2021, August 30). *Eight things you can do to improve your communication skills*. Professional Development | Harvard DCE. https://professional.dce.harvard.edu/blog/eight-things-you-can-do-to-improve-your-communication-skills/

Sheldon, R., & Wigmore, I. (2022, September). *What is pomodoro technique?*. WhatIs.com. https://www.techtarget.com/whatis/definition/pomodoro-technique

Sheppard, S. (2021, October 25). *How to build a respectful relationship*. Verywell Mind. https://www.verywellmind.com/respect-is-vital-to-building-a-healthy-relationship-5206110

Simeon, D. (2014, March 6). *Want your teen to be more organized? 10 ideas that actually work*. Your Teen Magazine. https://yourteenmag.com/teenager-school/teenager-middle-school/help-your-teenager-get-organized

Soukup, R. (2020, July 7). *How to stock your first kitchen*. Living Well Spending Less®. https://www.livingwellspendingless.com/how-to-stock-your-first-kitchen/

Srinivasan, H., & 2021. (2022, October 21). *When to use a debit card—and when to use a credit card instead*. Real Simple. https://www.realsimple.com/work-life/money/debit-vs-credit-card

Stickley, A. (2022, September 28). *The most effective ways to clean a garbage disposal*. The Spruce. https://www.thespruce.com/cleaning-a-garbage-disposal-2718863

Stretch your protein budget — nourish and exercise your body. (n.d.). Www.ag.ndsu.edu. Retrieved May 13, 2023, from https://www.ag.ndsu.edu/nourishyourbody/stretch-your-protein-budget

The importance of investing early and often. (n.d.). Associated Bank. https://www.associatedbank.com/resource-center/saving/investing-early-and-often

20 biggest time wasters for college students – college girl smarts. (2020, December 9). College Girl Smarts. https://www.collegegirlsmarts.com/biggest-time-wasters-for-college-students/

Types of abuse. (n.d.). The Hotline. https://www.thehotline.org/resources/types-of-abuse/

Vega, M. (2022, March 23). *Do you need an apartment co-signer? Apartment Living Tips*. ApartmentGuide.com. https://www.apartmentguide.com/blog/do-you-need-an-apartment-co-signer/

Wallender, L. (2022, June 17). *How to unclog any drain*. The Spruce. https://www.thespruce.com/how-to-unclog-a-drain-2718779

Washington state's mandatory auto/motorcycle insurance law. (n.d.). Office of the Insurance Commissioner Washington State. https://www.insurance.wa.gov/washington-states-mandatory-automotorcycle-insurance-law

Wells Fargo. (2022). *Why invest?* Wells Fargo. https://www.wellsfargo.com/goals-investing/why-invest/

What is a credit score? (2020, September 1). Consumer Financial Protection Bureau. https://www.consumerfinance.gov/ask-cfpb/what-is-a-credit-score-en-315/

What is renters insurance and what does it cover?. (2021, October). Allstate. https://www.allstate.com/resources/renters-insurance/what-does-renters-insurance-cover

Williams, R. (2019, March 28). *10 spiritual self-care tips to be happy.* Chopra. https://chopra.com/articles/10-spiritual-self-care-tips-to-be-happy

Wooll, M. (2022, January 11). *Why face-to-face communication matters (even with remote work).* BetterUp. https://www.betterup.com/blog/face-to-face-communication

Made in the USA
Monee, IL
29 May 2024

59081369R10099